DEEP DOMINATION

Bought by the Billionaire
Book Two

By Lili Valente

DEEP DOMINATION

Bought by the Billionaire
Book Two

By Lili Valente

Table of Contents

About the Book

WARNING: This is one deep, dark, hard-spanking, dirty-talking read. Are you ready?

Hannah is in too deep, falling steadily under Jackson's erotic control. It doesn't matter that he's her captor and tormentor. She lives for the nights when he draws her deeper into his world, teaching her the thrill of submission

Pain and pleasure. Love and hate. Him and her.

Jackson is falling—remembering why he couldn't get enough of the woman who destroyed him—but so is she. Soon, he'll reach Hannah's hard limit and her obedient façade will fall away, exposing the monster he's hunted across three continents.

But soon a shocking revelation interrupts

their dark and twisted game and Jackson is left wondering who is the true monster.

* * Deep Domination is the 2nd in the Bought by the Billionaire serial romance series. For maximum enjoyment it should be read after book one.* *

Author's Note

The Bought by the Billionaire series is a dark romance
with themes that may be disturbing to some readers.
Read at your own risk.

Dedicated to my Street Team, the sweetest bunch of naughty-hero-loving women around.

CHAPTER ONE

Six Years Ago
Jackson

Pulse leaping in his throat, Jackson jabbed Adam's contact profile on his phone, issuing orders the moment the other They had only been in the stuffy room at the end of the hall for half an hour, but Jackson was already sweating beneath his clothes and dangerously close to losing his shit.

The interrogation was a joke. It was clear, that in the minds of the two military police officers charged with getting his side of the story, he had already been tried and convicted.

1

He didn't know either of them, but they weren't hard to read. The older, red-headed man with the crooked nose wanted to pound Jackson unconscious and his partner—a young, fuzzy-haired brunette who barely looked old enough to have graduated from the academy—alternated between flushing red with anger and paling with disgust.

And fear. She was afraid of him, too.

He could see it in her eyes when her guard faltered. She was horrified by what she was certain he'd done. She was also scared of what might have happened to her if she'd encountered him on one of the more far-flung Quantico trails, deep in the forest where no one could have heard her scream as he'd forced himself on her.

As he'd *raped* her.

The thought made his stomach roil and bile rush up the back of his throat. He would *never* do that to a woman, *any* woman, let alone the woman he loved. Being questioned in connection with something like this was deeply disturbing, but the fact that he was accused of violating Harley was just...too much.

He felt dizzy, sick, and panicked, but also strangely above it all, like a ghost hovering in the air watching a man with dark circles under his eyes protest that he was innocent.

It was all so fucking bizarre.

He'd spent the past two days grieving Harley with an intensity that had left his insides black and blue, crying himself to sleep and wishing he never had to wake up again. All he wanted was for her to be alive, even if it meant she was married to Clay and he would never get to hold her again, never taste her skin or hear the breathy sound she made at the back of her throat as he pushed inside her.

He still loved her, and ached for her so deeply he worried the pain might kill him. He would never have hurt her—*never*.

He'd said as much to the MPs at least half a dozen times, but it bore repeating until these people got the message.

"It doesn't matter if anyone can confirm whether or not I was at home asleep four nights ago," he said, cutting off the red-haired officer in the middle of his latest monologue.

The man and his partner both had nametags on their uniforms, but Jackson couldn't seem to focus long enough to make sense of the letters stitched in black on gray. The entire morning had been too surreal, from the time the officers knocked on his front door to the moment he learned he was being questioned in connection with the rape of Harley Garrett.

"I didn't rape Harley. I love her." The reality that she was no longer alive to love hit him all over again, making it hard to swallow past the fist of emotion shoving up his throat.

"I loved her," he continued, his voice hoarse. "So much. I would never have hurt her. And if she were here right now she'd tell you that. She'd tell you everything we did was consensual."

"So you believe Miss Garrett was a truthful woman?" the female officer asked. She was pale now, not flushed, but Jackson was too frustrated to wonder if that was a good sign or a bad one.

"Yes," he said, shaking his head as he

realized that wasn't the truth, no matter how much he wanted it to be. "I thought so, anyway. She always seemed to be when we were together. But two days ago I learned that she was engaged to my best friend. They'd been dating behind my back for months so…"

He ran a clawed hand through his hair with a harsh sigh, trying not to think about the fact that Clay was gone, too. Clay, who had been his best friend since basic training and saved his life more than once. Clay, who would have been the first and only person he would have turned to at a time like this, the only person in his life he'd trusted with all of his secrets.

"So maybe she wasn't always truthful," he continued. "But she would have told you the truth about this."

"Why's that?" The woman—Pearson according to her name tag, though he would probably forget that the second he glanced away—lifted her unplucked brows. "Was she afraid to contradict you?"

Jackson balled his hands into fists on top of the table, fighting to keep the anger from his voice. "Because she was the one who wanted to experiment with being submissive. She's the one who wanted things rough." He lifted his chin and relaxed his fists, ignoring the doubt he could feel seething toward him from the other side of the table. "She wanted to take things even further, for me to gag her and use a whip that would leave marks on her skin, but I told her no."

"Why?" Pearson pressed.

"I wasn't ready to go that far until we had a serious commitment."

"You only hurt the ones you love?" the male officer asked with a barely controlled sneer.

"Because power exchange can be dangerous," Jackson said, not bothering to keep the condescension from his tone. "I've been involved in these kind of relationships before, but Harley was new to the lifestyle. I needed to know that she trusted me to take care of her and help her learn her limits. Like I said, I didn't want to hurt her."

He sat still, forcing himself to hold the gaze of first Pearson and then her older, meaner counterpart without flinching, resisting the urge to fill the silence. He'd offered enough explanation. If there was something they didn't understand, they could ask.

There was nothing perverted or wrong about what Harley had wanted—or in his need to make sure he was entering into a relationship in the way he felt was safest for a new-to-the-scene submissive. Giving your will over to another person for the first time can be overwhelming. Both the Dom and sub need to have similar expectations and be committed to working through the process together from the start.

He'd had doubts Harley was ready to submit to another person's control—she was so stubborn and didn't always seem to enjoy it when he started giving orders in the bedroom. But after the way she'd responded to him the night he'd climbed through her window, his doubts had faded away.

She had been so perfect, so vulnerable and honest and sexy as hell.

For the first time, he'd seen all the way to the heart of her, and known it was safe to tell her that he loved her. Because she loved him, too. She was scared and she had secrets and pain she tried so hard to hide, but deep down she was ready to take the first steps toward abandoning control. To him and only him. She was ready to hand over her power and let him help her find a way to be free of the things that haunted her.

As he'd kissed her goodbye he'd been certain they were on their way to something special.

Instead, it was the last time he would ever see her alive.

"I loved her," he said again, the words out of his mouth before he could stop them. "And now she's gone and I just…" He sucked in a shallow breath, willing himself not to break down. "I don't understand why this is happening."

"Maybe this will shed some light on that for you." Red turned to press play on the DVD player behind him.

The television sat on a dull gray portable stand and had already been in the room when Jackson was led in. He'd assumed it was part of the standard furnishings of the drab interrogation room, along with the chipped table, squeaky chairs, and the plastic water cooler in the corner.

But he'd been wrong. The television was there for him; he knew it the moment Harley's face flickered onto the screen.

His first reaction to seeing her tear-streaked face was joy—to see her again, to see her talking, animated, *alive*—followed closely by grief and then rage.

Someone had hurt her. Badly. Her face was swollen from crying and her big blue eyes darted back and forth, unable to look directly at the person questioning her on the other side of the table. She was trembling so badly he could hear the legs of her chair rattling on the floor, a soft, percussive accompaniment to her words.

To the nightmarish words spilling out of her pretty mouth.

Comprehension hit like a bolt of lightning, sudden and shocking. Jackson's lips parted, but no sound came. His throat closed and all the blood in his body seemed to rush away, leaving him drained and freezing in the room that, only a moment ago, had felt too warm.

But that was before he'd heard Harley describing a date on the beach they'd never had, before he'd watched her lifting her shirt to reveal bruises he hadn't given her. Before she'd sworn that he'd raped her again and again, until she could barely stand and had been forced to call an ex-boyfriend to drive her to the police station after Jackson allegedly left her bleeding in the sand.

He watched the tape in stupefied silence and remained mute for several long minutes after Pearson turned off the television and stopped the DVD.

How...

How could she? How could she have done this?

How could she have told such horrible lies about him when all he'd ever wanted to do was love and protect her?

There had to be some mistake, some explanation.

She was confused. That was it. It had been dark on the beach that night. Maybe she hadn't seen her attacker's face, maybe he'd grabbed her from behind or—

Stop it!

She knew your body, your touch. She would have known it wasn't you, even if she were blindfolded.

She's lying on purpose.

She's lying *on* purpose.

Finally, as his mind continued to echo the terrible truth over and over—like a scratched record stuck on repeat—and his heart continued to break he found his voice. "I didn't do it. She's lying. I don't know why, but it's all a lie."

Red leaned in, his brown eyes flat and cold. "You might want to rethink that line of defense. The DNA results from the rape kit came in last night. We pulled yours from the Marine database. They're an exact match."

Jackson shook his head, anger and confusion warring inside of him. "But we always used a condom. Every single time except..."

His eyes widened as the flaw in Harley's story suddenly became abundantly clear. "Those bruises were fake! Make-up or something. I saw her two nights ago, right before the crash. We slept together and she was fine. Every inch of her was clear and bruise-free. I swear there wasn't a mark on her."

"Do you have any evidence to support that?" Pearson asked, writing something in the tiny notebook she'd brought into the room, not even bothering to offer eye contact.

"No," he said, voice tight. "Why would I? I was with my girlfriend, who I thought was in love with me. I didn't think I'd have any reason to need to prove I hadn't beaten her to within an inch of her life."

He paused, watching Pearson show the note on her pad to Red, who nodded smugly.

"What is going on here?" Jackson asked, volume rising. "I'm being framed for a felony and you're buying a woman's lie without even giving me the benefit of the doubt. What the fuck is wrong with you?"

"Watch your mouth, soldier," Red said. "Everything you say in this room is admissible in court. You're the one who agreed to be questioned without an attorney."

Jackson clenched his teeth until his jaw was so tight it felt like the muscles were about to snap in two. "I've changed my mind," he finally ground out. "I want a lawyer. Now."

"We'll have a phone brought in for you. Might as well settle in, Staff Sergeant Hawke. You're going to be here for a while." Pearson smiled, a cold, victorious smile that made Jackson loathe her more than he did already, but not as much as he loathed Harley.

As much as he *should* loathe Harley.

She had conned him, played him, and framed him for a crime he didn't commit, but he couldn't bring himself to hate her.

Not that day. Or the next day, or the next.

But by the time he was sitting in a courtroom in front of a judge pronouncing him guilty of rape, he had begun to hate Harley Garrett with the same passion with which he'd loved her.

When the judge declared that he would be dishonorably discharged, stripped of all rank and pay, and sentenced to eighteen months in a military prison, the last ounce of his affection for Harley shriveled and died, leaving nothing in his heart except a burning hatred. His hatred was a roaring fire that he would stoke every day he spent behind bars, tempering himself in the flames until he was as heartless and remorseless as the woman who had ruined him.

The woman who had sentenced a man whose only crime had been loving the wrong girl to a fate worse than death.

He would never be the same. He would never love or trust anyone ever again. He would never be the man he was before.

That man was dead.

Harley had killed him and now all that was left was to return the favor.

CHAPTER TWO

Present Day
Hannah

Her stranger was clearly angry—furious—but Hannah couldn't have stopped the smile blossoming across her face if she'd tried.

It was really him, *him*, the man she'd tried to convince herself she wasn't obsessed with for six long years. The stranger who had laid claim to her body, captured her imagination, and haunted her dreams.

No…he had haunted her awakenings.

In her dreams, one glimpse of his face and she was electrified by pleasure. In dreams she was transported to the heaven of his arms, blessed by belonging to him in a way she'd never belonged to anyone, not even herself. It was waking up and realizing that the one night they'd shared had been a lie and that she would never see him again that was hell.

She'd always known that night was a lie, but now maybe he knew it too.

Maybe *that's* why he'd come for her. Her smile vanished so quickly it sent a flash of discomfort through her cheeks.

Hannah stared up at him, watching his jaw clench and storm clouds roll in behind his dark eyes. She cringed, wishing she could melt through the floor or that she at least had a blanket to pull across her body to shield her nakedness. But the polished hardwood held firm beneath her back and she remained exposed to her stranger, his release cooling on her bare chest as he glared down at her, his hands tightening into fists.

She half expected him to strike her, to drive his fist into her stomach as punishment for the smile she hadn't been able to control.

Instead, he squatted on his heels beside her,

moving with a slow, easy grace that sent a chill across her flesh. She felt hunted, but there was nowhere to run. He owned her. He had bought and paid for the privilege of enacting his revenge and now her life was in his hands.

He would decide whether the next month would pass in pleasure or pain.

He would decide how she would pay for her sins and whether she would leave this island alive.

The thought of him beating the life out of her with his large hands made her whimper, even before he brought one of them to her throat. His grip was loose, but his fingers were so long they completely encircled her neck, bringing her claustrophobia surging back with a vengeance, making her blood race and her head spin as he leaned down to whisper inches from her face.

"I will tell you this one time and one time only, so listen closely," he said, his voice thick with rage, but so smooth and controlled it somehow made his next words even more frightening. "I am not the man I was before.

There is no softness in my heart for you. There is no heart left to soften. I am beyond your reach. I own you and I intend to break you and nothing you do will change your fate. Do you understand?"

Hannah nodded as she swallowed convulsively, fighting to keep her breath under control as anxiety electrified her nerve endings.

"You can smile while I break you or you can cry," he continued, a smile curving his lips. "But the ending will be the same."

His grip tightened, not enough to hurt, but enough to make Hannah's anxiety creep toward full-blown panic. She was seconds from clawing at his fingers, when he suddenly released her and stood, wiping his hands on his neatly pressed pants, as if touching her had dirtied them in some way.

"Clean up. The bathroom should have everything you need," he said, pointing toward the opposite side of the room. "After you shower, you will stay in this room until granted permission to leave."

He turned to go, but stopped before he'd

taken five steps and spun back to face her, making Hannah's slowing pulse lurch back into high gear. "And if I learn you've disobeyed my order—any order I give you while you're here—all the promises I've made to you will be invalidated. Think about that before you try to run. Because I will find you, Harley, and my punishment will make it clear how gentle I've been with you so far."

Harley? Hannah's brows drew together, but she didn't say a word.

She didn't know what to say, what to think. She only knew that she wouldn't be able to organize her thoughts as long as he was in the room. His rage was a fire that sucked all the oxygen from the air and left her gasping, as shocked and confused as a fish dangling from the end of a fisherman's hook.

It wasn't until the heavy door closed behind him and she heard his footsteps moving away down the hall that she dared to drag her trembling body into a seated position. Her movement set his seed sliding down the front of her chest. A wave of self-loathing turned her stomach as memories of their brief time together raced through her head.

He must have thought she was Harley from the beginning. *That's* why he'd kept insisting that she say her name and been so angry when she maintained that she was Hannah North. She'd thought maybe he was one of her family's enemies and wanted confirmation that she was a Mason, not a North, but he'd been waiting for her to confess that she was her sister.

Somehow, he didn't know that her twin was dead and was clearly committed to punishing Harley for whatever sins she had perpetrated against him.

Hannah would have liked to believe her sister was innocent of whatever had turned her commanding, but once beautifully passionate, stranger into a terrifying man bent on revenge, but she knew better. She would always love her sister and grieve the fact that Harley had been taken away from her too soon, but she didn't believe in revisionist history.

Dying hadn't changed the person her twin

had been before she was murdered. And Harley had been a spiteful, inexorable, often frightening force of nature. She had played with men's hearts like a twisted child who enjoys torturing animals before putting the poor creatures out of their misery.

Their shared psychiatrist had said Harley's rough handling of romantic relationships was her way of protecting herself from becoming the kind of broken woman their mother had become, but that didn't make Harley's treatment any easier for her victims. Hannah had seen more than one strong man shattered after learning the woman he'd fallen in love with was an illusion and the reality was a sociopath who seemed to gain succor from breaking people's hearts.

Harley had always managed to walk away from the wreckage and disappear before her victim's grief could transform to rage. But now her sister's bad love karma had caught up with Hannah, who had been paid a million dollars to give a man a shot at vengeance.

Hannah couldn't tell her stranger the truth. If she told him that she was Harley's twin, not the woman who'd hurt him, she would endanger her and Sibyl's future.

He wouldn't want her if he learned the truth. Obviously a surrogate wouldn't suffice or he would have taken out his frustration on other women years ago. He wanted Harley, the "vindictive, psychotic bitch he'd bought" and no one else would do.

"What did you do to him, Harley?" Hannah whispered as she drew her knees in to her chest, shivering despite the evening sun streaming through the floor to ceiling windows behind her, warming the large room.

Sometimes Hannah would swear she could feel her sister's spirit lingering nearby, not ready to leave until they could go out of the world together, the way they'd come into it, but now the air remained quiet, empty. She was alone, defenseless, and had no choice but to play a dangerous game with a man incapable of compassion.

But maybe Harley didn't deserve compassion. Maybe she'd done something so horrible, so unforgivable that retribution was the only fitting response. And maybe Hannah would have no choice but to pay the price for Harley's mistakes.

As she came to her feet and padded silently toward the bathroom, she hoped she would find a way to survive being shattered by the only man who had ever made her dream about what it would be like to belong to someone—body and soul.

LILI VALENTE

CHAPTER THREE

Jackson

Jackson stormed out of the master bedroom and through the kitchen, where the petite housekeeper with the steel-streaked hair was in the middle of cooking something he dimly realized smelled wonderful.

But he was too angry with himself to pause to register anything good.

He'd come so close to losing it. The first time Harley threw him a curve ball, he'd nearly broken all the promises he'd made to himself.

A smile. A fucking *smile* was all it had taken

to set him back to dancing when she tugged his strings. He'd had six years to prepare and she'd nearly broken him two hours in.

But she didn't. You didn't let anger take control. And now you're prepared.

Now, you know better than to think this will be easy.

His thoughts slowed his racing pulse, but he didn't slow his pace toward the front of the house. He kept walking until he was striding down the wooden steps leading up to the lanai and down the gravel trail leading toward the sea. He needed to be alone with nothing but the sound of the waves crashing against the shore. He needed to stare at the place where rocks became sand and remember that steady and relentless wins out in the end.

Rocks may seem more durable than water. But the waves washing in and out, lapping away at stone year after year, eventually wear the largest rocks to pebbles, then to sand, and then to particles so small they might as well not exist at all. He didn't have years, but Harley wasn't a rock. She was slippery and quick, but she wasn't strong. A strong woman wouldn't need to lie, deceive, and shape shift the way she did. Deprived of her usual tools, she would begin to break down much faster than a stone losing its battle against the sea.

He just needed to maintain his focus and keep from getting swept up in any game but his own.

He reached the end of the road where gravel gave way to sand and stood watching the tide come in, the sea air whipping his hair from his face and filling his ears with the meditative rush of wind and waves.

The owners of the property warned their renters that the ocean on this side of the island was dangerous. The shore break was brutal, with waves that slammed into the steep incline where beach gave way to ocean with the force of a wrecking ball.

Even from a few dozen feet away, Jackson could feel the earth vibrating beneath his feet each time the ocean found its target. The first few feet of shoreline was pock-marked and jagged from the constant assault, but the sand farther up the beach remained untouched. It was mounded in peaceful dunes not found elsewhere on the island, where a gradual incline allowed the ocean to creep higher up the shore.

Brutality had its place, but its reach was limited and Jackson didn't want to hack away at Harley's protective shell. He wanted to creep past her outer defenses, through the sophisticated diversions she'd erected to deflect focus from her weakness, all the way to the deepest, most secret parts of her. He wanted to find the private places she held sacrosanct and rig the halls with explosives. He wanted to destroy her from the inside out, and for that he would need stealth and strategy, not a hand balled into a fist.

He was mentally running through his list of tactics and strategies, discarding those that seemed too blunt a tool to use now that he realized how quick and clever a viper he'd trapped under a basket, when his cell buzzed in his pocket.

Jackson pulled the slim phone free and glanced down to find a text from his spy—

Hoping you and Miss Hannah made it to your destination safely and will have a wonderful, relaxing vacation. I'll be keeping an eye on Miss Sibyl and will make sure she's taken care of. Please give Miss Hannah my best. She's a lovely girl.

Jackson's lips twisted. He tucked the phone into his pocket without bothering to respond.

Harley was only lovely on the outside and he couldn't care less what Hiro did with her aunt. The man had served his purpose and was no longer of any use to Jackson. But the pearl farmer's text did give him an idea...

Harley seemed to truly care about her family. She'd rarely spoken of her father, but when she'd mentioned her mother or aunt, her voice had softened in a way that had made the younger Jackson envious. Fool that he was, he'd wanted her voice to soften that way for him. He'd wanted to be part of her inner circle, to be one of the few people in the world who had touched her heart.

But Harley hadn't let him in that deep. She was selfish and guarded with her affections. Whether she was incapable of romantic love or she had simply hated him too much to find a reason to care about him, Jackson couldn't be sure, but he was positive he could use her love for her family against her.

He just needed to figure out how to sharpen the weapon and where to thrust the blade to do the most damage…

The thought had barely formed before he had his phone in his hand and Hiro's number on speed dial. When the other man answered Jackson spoke over his bright hello.

"I'd like you to get close to Sibyl North and see if you can find out her real last name," he said, turning away from the sea, sensing he had absorbed all the lessons it had to teach for the day. "Become her friend and confidante. I want private details of her life with Hannah, family pictures, stories, secrets they might be keeping, the location of other family members, anything you can find."

Hiro cleared his throat uncomfortably. "I don't know Mr. Hawke. I feel terrible about the lies I've told already. The ladies are good ladies. They are very sweet and gracious and I don't—"

"I'll triple your fee," Jackson said, cutting him off, unable to handle hearing anyone sing the praises of Harley Garrett. "I'll expect your first report in one week or I'll find someone else to do the job."

He hung up without waiting for the other man's response. Hiro would do as he was told. His flash of conscience would fade away in the face of the promise of more money. His family's pearl farm had yet to recover from the global recession and Hiro had three unwed sisters with eight children between them to feed. He would ingratiate himself into Sibyl North's life and hopefully report back with information Jackson would be able to use against Harley.

In the meantime, he would do what he did best—get up, brush himself off, and start again. He'd come too far to be thrown off course by a bump in the road. Harley was quick and clever, but he held all the cards.

Now it was just a matter of deciding which one to play first.

CHAPTER FOUR

Hannah

By the time Hannah emerged from her shower that first afternoon, her clothes had mysteriously vanished from the floor and none had appeared to take their place.

After an hour spent pacing the large master suite with nothing but a towel clutched around her breasts, Hannah searched the bureau drawers until she found a flowered sheet she managed to fashion into a toga. It wasn't much to look at—and she wasn't much to look at in it—but it covered her nakedness and stayed put better than the towel.

She expected her stranger to reappear sooner or later—hopefully with something for her to wear since she hadn't been allowed to bring a suitcase—but that first evening came and went without a sign of Mr. X or anyone else.

She woke Saturday morning to the sound of her stomach complaining and watched the sun shorten the shadows of the fruit trees in the expansive back lawn while her belly did its best to digest itself. She was a few minutes from violating the order not to leave her room to go in search of food when a small, nut-brown woman with gray threading through her long black braid pushed into the room carrying a breakfast tray.

The smell of hot buttery croissants, freshly cut fruit, and hot coffee in its own tiny French press was enough to make Hannah dizzy with gratitude. At least starvation wasn't to be part of her punishment.

"Thank you so much," she said, smiling as the woman set the tray down on the low table near the window. "I'm Hannah. Have you worked here long?"

"Eva," the woman said, her expression guarded. "No English."

Refusing to be deterred, Hannah widened her smile and made her introduction again in French, the language of most Tahitians, but Eva didn't seem to understand that either. Hannah was getting ready to try in Spanish, when a man's voice spoke softly from behind them.

"Mami, tu saves muy bien que no tienes nada de hablar con esa mujer."

Hannah turned to see the owner of the voice—a tall, slim dark-haired man with expressive eyes and a full mouth—motioning urgently for Eva to exit the room.

"Why aren't you supposed to speak to me?" Hannah tailed the older woman as she hurried across the room. "Please," she said, reaching out a hand to hold the door open after Eva had slipped beneath the man's arm and disappeared down the hall. "Please, I just want someone to talk to. I'm not dangerous."

"But the man we work for is." Up close, the kid looked even younger. He couldn't be more than twenty-one, but there was a dark knowledge in his gaze that made it clear he'd seen more than most men twice his age. "So we'll do what Mr. Hawke says. You will be smart to do the same."

He turned and walked away before Hannah could recover from the excitement of being granted a piece of the puzzle.

Mr. Hawke. She had a last name!

Unless someone else owns this island. Maybe a friend of Mr. X's, who is as dangerous and insane as his houseguest.

The voice of doom had a point, but Hawke fit her stranger. It seemed apropos that he would be named after a bird of prey.

If she'd had a few more minutes with Eva or her son, she might have been able to confirm that her abductor was their employer. She might have even learned his first name, which she would need as soon as she gained access to a computer or cell phone.

She paced back and forth in front of the partially open door, thoughts racing, determined to make contact with the son again at the first opportunity. He was concerned for his mother, but he seemed kind, too. At least kind enough that he had spared the time to give her a word of warning. She sensed that he could be valuable to her if she could gain his sympathy. At the very least he might help her keep from losing her mind.

Hannah didn't want to get anyone in trouble, but she needed human connection. She needed to ground herself in this world via someone other than her stranger. If he was her only contact with humanity, she feared it wouldn't be long before she lost what remained of her composure.

Her shoulders bunching with frustration, she shut the door and crossed back to her breakfast. She ate the two croissants and all of the fruit salad—she didn't know when she would be fed again and it made sense to fill up—but the delicious baked goods and aromatic coffee didn't taste as good as they should have. Anxiety left a bitter flavor in her mouth that tainted every bite.

If someone had asked her yesterday, she would have insisted there was nothing worse than having her stranger standing over her naked body with murder in his eyes. But this…waiting for the other shoe to fall, for the first shot to be fired, for the monster to leap out from behind the trees with claws bared, was so much worse.

She spent most of her first full day on the private island pacing her bedroom, staring out at the sunny day beyond the back patio off the master suite, growing progressively agitated. She had no work, no books, no television, no radio, not even a pack of cards to keep her mind focused on something other than the fact that she was the prisoner of a dangerous man who intended to destroy her.

Dread was slowly driving her out of her mind, a fact she was sure Hawke—if that was his name—was well aware of. He clearly had no moral compass to prevent him from using every dirty psychological trick in the book to weaken her defenses.

But he'd imprisoned a former psychology student, not a sculptor with a well-documented anxiety disorder. Hannah knew all about Stockholm Syndrome and she refused to fall victim to it. She would not mistake the absence of cruelty for kindness, she would not empathize or identify with her captor. She would remain focused on her deepest sense of self and her right to human decency.

Even if she were Harley and had done something worthy of punishment, she would still deserve that much. Even criminals on death row were allowed to eat, exercise, read, and lift their face to the sun for a few hours each week.

As soon as Hawke returned, she would demand that she be allowed a book and the right to walk outside in the back yard. She would make him see that she deserved a reward for her obedience.

He wants to push you into a breakdown, Hannah. You'll be lucky if you're not tortured, let alone rewarded.

Her thoughts were chilling, but she refused to dwell on them. She had to remain in the moment and face challenges as they arose. If she let herself start imagining all the things he might do to her, she would be doing his work for him and she refused to be complicit in her own destruction.

She went to bed that night determined to stay strong and woke the next morning three times as stir crazy as before. By the time she'd eaten her breakfast and the equally delicious lunch Eva delivered—scurrying in and out of the room so quickly it would have been funny if Hannah didn't know the poor woman's speed was born out of terror—she was near the end of her rope.

Not only was her captivity mind-numbingly boring, it gave her far too much time to think.

For the past six years, she'd been so busy struggling to keep the bed and breakfast afloat and scrambling to recover from one tragedy after another that she hadn't had time to dwell on how empty her life was in so many ways.

But now, with nothing but four silent walls to stare at, she had time to think about the dreams she'd abandoned in the name of survival. She'd never finished her education or opened the children's therapy practice she'd dreamed about since she was eleven years old. She'd never met a man who loved everything about her—the strong and the weak, the sweet and the sour—or started a family. She'd never been able to find out if she would have been a better parent than her cold father or shadow of a mother and now her dreams might never come true.

What if Hawke intended to do more than break her? What if he decided to end her life, here on this island where no one would lift a finger to help her?

And even if he let her live, was she strong enough to survive the kind of mental abuse he had in mind? Would she look back on these long lonely days later and curse herself for being too afraid to run for her life? Should she at least step far enough outside to get a better idea of where she was?

She stood at the sliding door leading out onto the patio, her mouth flooding with saliva and her palms and bare feet itching. She could practically taste how good the sea air would feel on her skin and the cushion of carefully manicured grass beneath her feet. She wanted to go outside so badly her bones ached with the need for freedom and movement and sun on her face, but she couldn't fight the feeling that he was watching and would know the moment she disobeyed his order.

His quiet threat that his promises would be revoked if she violated his commands was all that kept her from throwing open the door and racing across the lawn.

She was as terrified of rape as any other woman, but she was even more terrified of being raped by him, the man who had given her the greatest pleasure she'd ever known. It would be even more heinous and unbearable. It would be seeing something holy and beautiful mutilated and covered in blood.

She was quickly growing to fear Hawke, but she still treasured the memory of that one night and the pleasure he'd given her.

You'd better get over that, Hannah. Fast. You're giving him power he doesn't deserve.

"Easier said than done," she muttered as she paced away from the window, deliberately refraining from looking at the place on the floor where he'd driven her crazy before releasing himself on her bare breasts.

She'd replayed every moment of that encounter at least a dozen times in the past two days, looking for clues to what he had planned for her, but each time all she'd succeeded in accomplishing was making her body long for his touch. He was terrifying, out of his mind, and dangerous, but he was also the sexiest man she'd ever met.

It was sick, but during her shower that night, she couldn't keep from imagining that the fingers slipping between her thighs were his. She craved his touch almost as much as she craved a break from the anxiety soaked air inside her makeshift prison. She craved release, too, but after several long minutes of sliding her fingers through where she pulsed and ached, it became obvious she wasn't going to be able to find it.

Her mind was afraid to violate his order not to make herself come while they were on the island. And her body didn't want her soft touch. It wanted him, his rough hands and commanding voice ordering her to come.

With a soft curse, she shut off the water and dried off with hands shaking from denied satisfaction. She brushed her teeth with her eyes fixed on the marble countertop, refusing to look her pathetic reflection in the mirror, and crept in to curl under the covers fighting the urge to sob.

She had barely spoken more than a few sentences to anyone in two days. It wasn't that long in the scheme of things, but she felt so profoundly alone. She was unraveling faster than she would have thought possible.

For years, she'd been the shoulder her aunt could lean on, and had been Harley's steadying force long before that. She'd thought she was strong, but he was proving how wrong she'd been.

She should hate him for it, for ripping off her blinders and showing her all the cracks in her armor, but she couldn't stop thinking about the last time she'd seen Harley.

Her sister had been up to something, and Hannah's gut had insisted it was something bad. There was a chance that her stranger had been her twin's last victim and had every right to be hurt and angry. But how would Hannah ever convince him that she'd learned the error of her ways if she had no idea what Harley had done to him?

"His name," she whispered to herself,

curling more tightly under the covers, her overly sensitive nerve-endings irritated by the feel of the sheets against her bare skin. "Start with his name and go from there."

If she could learn the rest of his name, she'd have something to type into a search engine the moment she had access to a computer. His name was the first step.

That's all she should focus on, taking one step at a time until she found a way to survive this nightmare with her mind intact.

CHAPTER FIVE

Hannah

On the fourth night of her captivity, after more long fear-laced days of monotony and going to bed with tears running down her cheeks, Hannah was awoken by her own groan of relief.

She sucked in a breath and held it, her eyes blinking fast as she peered into the near darkness. For a moment, she had no idea where she was, but then she saw the palm trees waving in the moonlight outside the window, heard the gentle rustle of their leaves in the breeze, and felt big, strong hands hot on her breasts.

Waking up fast, she breathed into the fingers playing with her nipples. Her stranger plucked and teased at her swollen flesh, sending fissures of excitement washing through her. After days of silence and solitude, his touch was a glass of water in the desert.

"You awake, princess?" he asked, his lips moving against her bare neck, sending another rush of awareness sweeping across her skin.

"Yes." She moaned as her bare bottom brushed against where he was hot and hard. He had crept naked and uninvited into her bed in the middle of the night and touched her without her consent. She should be scared or angry, but all she felt was relief and she was too worn down by loneliness to fight it.

Besides, there was nothing to be gained by lashing out. She needed to arouse his empathy, not remind him why he wanted to punish her.

"You feel so good," she said, teeth digging into her bottom lip as he intensified his efforts, rolling her erect nipples until she squirmed in the circle of his arms.

He thrust forward, pressing his thickness between her ass cheeks. "So you've missed me, then?"

"Yes." She arched her back, tilting her hips until her wetness brushed against the base of his erection.

He was as massive as she remembered. His cock was so thick and long she would be afraid he would do her damage if she hadn't already experienced the harmony of how perfectly they fit together. She knew there was nothing better than the feel of him buried to the hilt, filling her up until there was nothing but him, nothing but pleasure so intense it was almost painful.

"You missed this?" One of his warm hands slid down her stomach and between her legs, setting her on fire.

His fingers circled her swollen clit, bringing her body even more fiercely to life. She was tempted to let go and get lost in the bliss he sent cascading through her, but she had to come away from this night with something she could use.

She had to learn his full name. It would give her a reason to hope, something to hold on to as he continued to do his best to break her.

"Yes, sir," she said, heart leaping as he hummed softly in approval. "I'm sorry I smiled."

He grunted. "Is that right? Why are you sorry?"

"Because it made you angry," she said, circling her hips, grinding back against his cock as his skilled fingers drove her higher. "Because it made you leave."

"You're wrong," he said, a smile in his voice. "I set my own course, princess. I've just been too busy to spare time for you. I have a business to run."

"What kind of business?" she asked.

"The kind wrongly convicted criminals turn to after their lives are ruined," he said, pleasantly. "Illegal business. Bad business." He pinched her nipple harder, sending a sharp wave of pleasure pain coursing through her and drawing a gasp from her throat. "Turn over."

Before Hannah could obey—or properly digest the fact that she was in bed with an ex con—he flipped her onto her back and roughly nudged her legs open with his knee. His touch wasn't gentle, but that wasn't what she wanted from him. Her twisted libido craved his rough use.

Fresh heat rushed from her body as he reached down, using his thumbs to spread her sex wide. "I love how wet you get. I love that I can smell how much you want me to fuck you."

"Yes," Hannah said, anticipation making her shiver. "But first I want to give you what you asked for."

"What's that?" he asked, his gaze still directed down at her pussy, though she wasn't sure how much he could see in the dim moonlight drifting through the window.

"Marlena Renee." She gasped as he plunged his thumb into where she ached, but fought to keep her thoughts on track. "That's my name. My parents tried to call me Marley, but I insisted on being called Harley instead."

"Why's that?" he asked, setting a steady rhythm in and out of her body that threatened to destroy her ability to concentrate on anything except how much she wanted him.

"I thought Marley sounded like a dog's name," she said, leaving out that Harley had also been firm in her belief that twins should have names that started with the same first letter.

Harley was only six years old when she'd informed their parents that she would be Harley Mason from now on and that they should take the steps needed to facilitate the change, including ordering a new monogrammed pillow for her and Hannah's shared princess canopy bed.

Their mother had fought her at first—Marlena was a family name dating back five generations—but Harley had won out in the end. Harley always won in the end, a thought Hannah drew strength from as she tried to channel her twin's cunning.

"What about you?" she asked, lifting into his thrusts. "What was the name on your birth certificate?"

"Jackson Xavier Hawke," he said, but his next words banished the thrill of her small victory. "But you can call me sir. We won't be on a first name basis while we're here, Harley, and you're mistaken if you think stories about your childhood will make me rethink what I plan to do to you."

"I didn't," she said softly. "I just wanted to please you."

"Then you should roll over and get on your hands and knees." He sat back on his heels, watching her calmly, clearly certain that she would obey.

But suddenly Hannah wasn't feeling in the mood to be a good girl. Being a good girl had gotten her nothing except trapped in this room and driven half out of her mind with desire, fear, and frustration.

Compliance was failing her. It was time to see what defiance would do.

"No," she said, scooting back toward the headboard, gasping as he grabbed her behind the knees and jerked her beneath him.

"That word isn't in your vocabulary when you're speaking to me," he said, capturing her wrists in his hands and forcing them above her head, pinning them to the mattress. "Especially when we're in bed. You will say yes sir or nothing at all. Now get on your hands and knees."

"Go fuck yourself." The words sent a giddy rush through her overheated skin. She had never spoken that way to anyone, but this man brought out all kinds of unexpected sides of her.

"No, I'm going to fuck *you*," he said, dropping his hips and grinding his hot length against the top of her. His erection slid through her slick folds, teasing her swollen clit, but she refused to let the pleasure he sent rushing through her show on her face.

"I thought you were going to make me beg," she said, glaring up at him. "I don't hear any begging, do you?"

"No, I don't," he said with a smile. His lips were so close she could smell the smoky, astringent smell of bourbon on his breath and wondered how much he'd had to drink before he had come to her bed. If he'd had too much, he might not remember his promises, or care about honoring them if he did.

Her jaw tightened and her captive's hands balled into fists as he kneed her legs wider and shifted his hips, bringing the thick head of his cock to press against her entrance. She tensed against him, though she knew that would make it hurt like hell when he pushed inside. He was obscenely long and thick, almost more than she could accommodate even dripping wet and eager, but she refused to make this easy for him.

"Then beg me, Harley," he whispered, nudging ever so gently against her wetness. "Beg me to fuck you."

"I'd rather you go to hell," she said, pushing on before he could respond. "If you're going to rape me, at least use a condom. I'm not on any birth control."

His hands tightened around her wrists until her bones began to ache and murder flashed behind his eyes, but after a moment he lifted his hips, moving his erection away from her entrance. "You think I want to doom an innocent baby to having *you* for a mother?" he asked in a cold whisper. "You think I would do something like that to my own child?"

She swallowed, but didn't know how to respond or how to make sense of the shame that washed through her.

"I have respect for life, Harley. Just not yours," he continued. "I also have a condom on the bedside table. Now shut your mouth and get on your hands and knees or I promise you will be very sorry."

Electricity flashed across her skin and sweat broke out on her upper lip. Her gut screamed for her to obey. If she did, he would keep his promise to make her beg, to make her feel good for a little while before he made her feel bad again. No matter how angry, confused, and frustrated she was, she sensed that she could trust him to keep his promises.

He was angry, but he was in control. It was one of the things that had devastated her the first time they'd made love. He was deliciously in command of himself and his lover, Dominant in a way that made her feel safe giving herself to him completely, trusting him to catch her if she got so lost in pleasure that she couldn't find her way back to her body again.

But he was not the man he'd been the first time they were together. He didn't care about her and she couldn't trust him as far as she could throw him. Which, considering he was twice her size, with muscles on top of muscles and a powerful body chiseled to a cruel kind of perfection, wouldn't be very far.

So instead of rolling over like an obedient mouse, she lifted her chin and whispered, "No."

The moment the words passed her lips, she realized she had made a serious mistake. Because her words made him smile, a dangerous smile that promised pain.

CHAPTER SIX

Jackson

Suddenly the fog clouding Jackson's thoughts burned away and the path forward was perfectly clear.

He'd been going about this all wrong. Isolation and unpredictable, erotic visits at all hours of the night might throw the average woman off her game, but Harley wasn't average. And she wasn't the kind of enemy who could be bested by planning and forethought. Trying to catch her in a trap like that was like trying to swat flies with a fifty-pound cinder block.

She would see him coming and dart away every time. She was too quick, too determined, and too malleable.

Harley's biggest strength was in how swiftly she could read a person and adapt her behavior to get what she wanted from them. Whether it was kindness, hate, fear, or sympathy, Harley was skilled in eliciting the responses she needed. And for some reason, tonight she'd decided she wanted to make him angry, to push him into breaking his promises and taking her by force.

But he wasn't the fool he'd been six years ago. He refused to let her under his skin or allow her to call the shots. He was in control and he was going to make that abundantly clear.

"All right." He rolled off the bed, flicking on the bedside lamp before reaching for the black silk pajama pants he'd left on the floor when he climbed into her bed. "Then I'll go get your clothes and tell Adam you're ready to leave."

She sat up, clutching the sheet to her chest as she blinked in the glow of the lamp.

"What?"

"If you refuse to obey, then you will forfeit the rest of your fee and we'll find another way to settle our unfinished business." He stepped into his pants and pulled them up to his hips, tucking his still raging erection beneath the waistband. He might be putting Harley on a plane and heading to bed with a killer case of blue balls, but he doubted it.

She sat up straighter. "But I don't—"

"One hundred thousand dollars won't save your property. It won't even put a dent in the repairs that need to be done," he cut in as he grabbed the open condom sitting on the box beside the bed and tossed it into the trashcan on the other side of the bedside table. "Especially when I make sure not a single skilled laborer on the island is willing to work for you or your aunt and not a real estate agent who values his or her life will show the property. For any amount of commission."

"You can't do that," she protested, but it was clear she feared he could.

"Money can buy anything," he said with a pointed look. "People are always for sale and usually more affordable than one would think."

"But my aunt is innocent," Harley said, desperation creeping into her tone. "She's done nothing to deserve this."

"I think we've both proven we don't give a damn about guilt or innocence. It will only be a matter of time until your business folds and when it does I'll be waiting for you to end up penniless on the street." He started calmly toward the bedroom door, throwing his parting shot over his shoulder. "And you can trust that my offer of assistance will be much less generous the second time around."

"Wait," she called out. "Please wait…sir."

It obviously pained her to speak the last word, which made her submission all the sweeter.

He paused, but didn't turn. "Yes?"

"I'm sorry," she said. "I'll do what you asked. I'll do whatever you say."

"I'm not sure I believe you." He sighed, keeping his back to her so she couldn't see the satisfied look on his face. "You'll have to show me."

"I will, I promise. Whatever you want, sir."

He turned, electricity prickling across the surface of his skin as he faced his prey. "Whatever I want and exactly when I want it. You will not say no to me again, or the choice to leave will no longer be yours."

He started toward her, closing the distance between them with slow, deliberate steps. "You will obey me and submit to me. And what's more, you will make me believe you enjoy your submission, that you are eager and desperate to service me."

She swallowed, her throat working visibly as she nodded.

"I can't hear you, Harley," he said, stopping inches from the bed, forcing her to tilt her head back to look him in the face.

"Yes, sir," she whispered.

"Yes, sir, what?" he pressed. "What are you going to do to please me, pet?"

"Whatever you say, whenever you say it," she said, the light in her eyes dying a little with every word she spoke. "And I will make you believe that I'm enjoying it."

He smiled as he reached out to cup her

cheek in his hand. "Very good."

"Thank you, sir," she said, trembling as he ran his fingers up and down her elegant throat. He was tempted to tell her she was doing a shit job of pretending so far, but he was enjoying her fear too much to play that particular chip right now.

"But if you defy me again, you will find yourself back on that plane faster than you can say lying whore," he said, still smiling as he ran his fingers into her hair and made a fist, drawing a gasp from her throat as he gave her head a gentle shake for emphasis. "Is that understood?"

"Yes, sir," she said, shoulders cringing closer to her ears.

"Good." He released her and pointed toward the bottom of the bed. "Get up. Off the bed, with your feet on the ground and your hands on the footboard."

Harley tossed off the sheet and scrambled off the bed, hurrying to do his bidding so quickly her full breasts bounced as she moved. He enjoyed the show, watching her bend over, assuming the position.

"Feet farther back," he corrected. "And a deeper bend at the waist."

She obeyed, making his cock twitch with appreciation. But it wasn't time for that. Not yet. Not until she'd had her punishment and proved to him how much she enjoyed it.

"Your punishment will be a spanking," he said, slowly circling the bed, admiring the way the submissive posture emphasized the curves of Harley's body.

He wanted to bite the swell where her waist became her ass, to reach beneath her body to pinch and tease her nipples, and finally to plunge his fingers into her wet cunt, stretching her before he replaced his fingers with his cock. But from now on, she would have to earn her pleasure with pain and degradation she would learn to suffer with a smile.

"I'm going to give you the spanking you used to beg me for, do you remember?" He came to stand beside her, running his palm down her right buttock to her thigh.

"Y-yes," she said. "Yes, sir."

"A spanking that will leave you aching and swollen," he continued, caressing her left buttock as well, letting his palms run up and down, warming the soft flesh. "That will leave marks on your skin and make you think of me every time you sit down for the next few days."

She shivered and her muscles tensed beneath his hands, but she didn't speak a word.

"And you are going to enjoy it, aren't you, princess?" he asked. "Because you're getting what you wanted."

"Yes, sir." She sucked in a breath and he suspected she was fighting back tears, but he didn't care. He had no pity for her, not any more than she'd had for him when she'd painted her body to make it look like he'd beaten her black and blue.

The thought gave him a wonderful idea...

"You will keep your hands on the bed until I tell you otherwise and count the blows with me," he said, still stroking her, knowing the gentle way he was touching her now would only make what was to come more shocking. "We will count to fifty, the number of times I would have had to strike you for you to earn all those bruises you faked before you went to the police."

She stilled. "Sir?"

"It's all right." He braced one hand on the baseboard beside hers as he leaned in to whisper in your ear. "I don't blame you." He reached beneath her, rolling her nipple idly between his finger and thumb. "I blame the idiots who were too stupid to tell a real victim from a fake one."

Her breath rushed out. "Well, I...I'm sorry anyway, sir. I really am."

He laughed as he pinched her nipple tighter. "We both know that's not true, but it will be." He captured her other nipple, plucking it once, twice, three, times before he added in a whisper. "Besides, I was lying, too. I do blame you, and I'm going to show you just how much."

He stepped back, ignoring her whimper as he kicked her ankles farther apart, widening her stance, baring her pussy to him along with her ass. He was surprised to find a hint of slickness glistening at her entrance, but not displeased. He didn't give a damn if she enjoyed this. Let her. If she got off on being punished, that was fitting, because he was certainly going to get off on delivering the punishment.

He brought his left hand to her waist, curling his fingers around her hip in a tight grip to brace himself. "Count with me. If you stop or lose track, we'll start again from the beginning."

"Yes, s—" Her words ended in a bleat of surprise as his right hand made stinging contact with her right buttock.

"I didn't hear a one," he said, admiring the red handprint already rising on her pale flesh. "So we'll start again."

He let his hand fly, delivering a stinging slap to her left buttock. This time, her cry ended with a strained—

"One!"

He struck her again—hard, with the full flat of his palm and she bleated out, "Two" in the same slightly shocked voice. By the time they reached "Ten" and "Eleven" she was fighting to draw an even breath. By the time she gasped "Twenty-Five" her entire backside was swollen and her knees were shaking as she fought to hold herself upright.

By "Thirty-eight" welts were rising on her flesh and her skin was such an angry red he might have felt a little guilty for assigning such a high number of blows if she wasn't the woman who had sent him to jail.

And if her pussy wasn't so wet he could smell her arousal sweet and salty in the air.

He was hurting her—he had no doubt about that, this was never intended to be a teasing kind of spanking—and she was loving it. Not pretending to love it, not faking a smile or an aroused moan, but dripping down her thighs, swollen and wet and dying for him to fuck her, loving it.

He'd known going into this venture that Harley was disturbed, but even he hadn't expected her to be this messed up. But she was legitimately turned on by being spanked by the man she'd sent to prison.

The only thing more disturbing was how much he wanted to drive his throbbing cock between her flaming ass cheeks. His hand was shaking by the time he reached the fiftieth blow, but it wasn't from exhaustion. It was from the mind-numbing need to fuck her, to get his cock in her dripping cunt as fast as humanly possible.

As soon as the spanking was finished, he shoved his pajama pants down and stepped out of them, leaving the fabric in a pool beside Harley's feet as he headed for the bedside table. He ripped the condom open with his teeth, rolling it onto his cock as he returned to Harley's side. He was so swollen that veins stood out along his length and he could barely force the rubber over the blue head of his cock. He was more turned on than he'd been in years, dying to fuck Harley until she screamed, but he needed to hear two words first.

"Harley, do you want me to fuck you now?" he asked, his balls aching even more fiercely when she arched her back, presenting her wet pussy as she moaned in a low, shamed voice—

"Yes, sir. Please, sir. Please!"

With a savage smile born of beating his fucked up little bitch at her own game,

Jackson gripped her full hips in his hands and slammed home.

LILI VALENTE

CHAPTER SEVEN

Hannah

Hannah screamed as he plunged inside her, forcing his thickness all the way to the end of her channel. The blunt head of his cock collided with the end of her womb, triggering a sharp twinge of pain that made her cry out in satisfaction.

Even though it hurt. Even though it was hurt upon hurt.

God. What had he done to her?

This was so good, so bad, so twisted and sick, but also exactly what she wanted. What she needed.

She was lost in sensation, helpless to control herself. Gripping the base of the bed for dear life, she pushed her stinging, swollen ass backwards as he plunged into her again, filling her with his need, stretching her until her pussy burned. She craved the feel of his lightly furred thighs bumping against her abused flesh. She relished the way his fingers and thumbs bit into the fullness of her hips as he rode her hard and fast, driving them both toward the brink.

She moaned in abandon and spread her legs farther apart, welcoming him deeper, wanting more pain, more pleasure.

When he'd told her how she was to be punished, she'd been afraid, not turned on. She'd had fantasies about spanking before, but never as a way to illustrate that she was beneath a man, beneath his consideration, a whore he would use the way he saw fit. But by the second slap, she'd known there would be no fighting the waves of arousal rushing across her skin, tightening her nipples until they stung.

The blows sent thick, sticky desire

spreading through her core, until blood rushed to the places where he struck her, making her engorged sex plump and sensitive. He'd hit her with the flat of his hand, with enough strength to hurt, making it clear this wasn't about mutual pleasure, but it didn't matter. The pain summoned pleasure and together they banished the fear and anxiety that had been plaguing her for days.

For the first time since they'd arrived on the island, she wasn't living half in the terrifyingly uncertain future. She was completely in this moment, this spell-binding, mind-numbing moment, where she was getting fucked so hard her stinging ass rippled with every rough stroke of Jackson's cock. She was soaking wet and her pelvis filled with blood, heat, and that heavy feeling that spread through her core just before release.

But this build was so much more intense than anything she'd ever felt before. This was a sledgehammer swinging straight at her soul, ready to shatter everything that made her Hannah apart. This was more than submission, this was abandon, this was reckless and dangerous and afterward she might never be the same.

As the orgasm crept closer, she began to shake, afraid of the wave of pleasure now that it was so close there would be no escape from it, but she was helpless to hold it at bay. The next time Jackson's cock rammed home she screamed again, her legs buckling as ecstasy unlike anything she'd ever experienced rocketed through her, ricocheting through her body like a bullet fired in a steel room.

She fell to the floor and he followed her, kneeling behind her, his urgent rhythm growing frantic as he pushed through her pulsing flesh, forcing her to accept him even as her pussy clenched down so hard it felt like she might squeeze him in half.

This hurt, too. It hurt and it was perfect. It was wicked and it was wonderful. She didn't know up from down, right from wrong, or anything for certain except that when Jackson grabbed a fistful of her hair and wrenched her head back as he came inside her with a roar, there was nothing to do but call his name as she came again.

The second orgasm was fire licking across her flesh, singeing her nerve endings, leaving scars behind as her soul was forced from her skin and bones by the strength of her pleasure. She would never be the same. She would *never* be the same. Never.

She knew it was true, even before she came back to herself enough to realize that she was muttering the words beneath her breath, while Jackson stroked a slow, easy hand down her sweat-soaked back.

"Never," she whispered, gulping hard as she tried to stop the flow of words and failed. "Never the same."

"Shh," Jackson said gently, still stroking her feverish skin. "You're safe. It's all right."

She shivered. She wasn't safe. She was far, far from safe. She'd just had an out-of-body experience triggered by a hard spanking and a harder fucking from a psychopath. But something in Jackson's tone and that soft touch from his often cruel hand helped her calm down enough to regain control.

"I'm sorry, sir," she finally said, surprised to find tears rising in her eyes.

"Why are you sorry?" He continued to pet her, helping her come back to her body, making her aware of the fact that his softening cock was still buried inside of her.

"I let go of the bed," she whispered.

"You did," he said. "You also came without permission."

"Oh." Hannah risked a glance over her shoulder. "I forgot about that part."

"You're a very bad girl," he said, running his hand over the swollen flesh of her ass as he pulled out and guided the condom off of his cock. "Very bad."

Now that she could see her own skin, she was amazed that the spanking hadn't hurt more. Her bottom was the bright, lobster red of a tourist's sunburn. It was going to ache like hell tomorrow, and there might even be bruises under that enflamed skin, but right now, there was no pain.

Right now she couldn't feel anything but a floating, helplessly satisfied feeling unlike anything she'd felt before. Even with Jackson that night in her sister's bed. She was high on what they'd done and already craving another fix.

"Will you have to punish me again sir?" she asked, shocked by the erotic invitation implicit in her breathy whisper.

She was even more shocked when Jackson smiled, a beautiful, pleased-with-her smile that made her want to please him again. Again and again, no matter what an insufferable maniac he was or how much she feared that pleasing him wouldn't be enough to keep him from driving her out of her mind.

"Yes, I'm going to have to punish you again," he said, sending a thrill of excitement racing through her. "I'm going to have to punish you until you remember to follow the rules. Now turn around, lie down, and spread your legs. We're going to teach you how not to come."

"Yes, sir." Hannah obeyed, fresh heat rushing from her well-used pussy as he brought his hands to the backs of her legs and spread them wide.

CHAPTER EIGHT

Hannah

Hannah held her breath as she gazed down the landscape of her own body at the gorgeous man kneeling between her thighs, suddenly wishing things were different, wishing this was only a kinky encounter instead of a hopelessly fucked up one.

Jackson was heart-stopping like this, a man in his element, in complete control. If things were different, she could quickly become addicted to this version of Jackson and all the viciously wonderful things he made her feel.

"There is only one rule of cunt licking

club," he said, a wicked twinkle in his eye as he lowered his face between her legs.

"What's that, sir?" she asked, clit swelling as she imagined what it would feel like to have his mouth on her.

"You do not talk about cunt licking club," he said, the joke taking her by surprise. "And you don't come until I tell you to."

Before she could say "yes, sir" his tongue was driving so deep into her pussy it made her sex clench and her back arch off the cool floorboards beneath her.

He cupped her stinging ass in his hands, leveraging her closer to his mouth, banishing the pain that flashed through her abused flesh with the magic he worked with his tongue. Hannah's hands fisted at her sides and her eyes rolled back as he flicked and jabbed, showing her just what she'd been missing with men who were mere tourists in the land of cunnilingus.

Jackson teased her clit with feather light brushes before thrusting into her pussy and curling the thick muscle, caressing her inner walls in a come hither movement that had her pressing her heels into the earth, desperate to get closer to his mouth. She groaned as he pushed deeper, hitting some previously undiscovered place inside her that made her pussy weep for more of him.

"Easy," he murmured, withdrawing his magnificent tongue just as the tension building within her began to peak. "Take slower, deeper breaths."

She sucked in a deeper breath, but slower was much harder. She was already so close to the brink she could feel the hot desert wind of oblivion blowing in her face, tempting her to throw her arms wide and fly.

But this wasn't about pleasure, this was about control and she was determined to show him she had as much will power as he had.

Fingernails digging into her palms she forced herself to blow out through her pursed lips for three seconds and then to sip air in through her nose for another three. But yoga breath only took her so far.

As soon as he resumed his wicked work— kissing and nibbling the quivering flesh on either side of her entrance, his attention to that usually neglected area making her even more sensitive when he brought his tongue back to her clit—she was quickly back at the razor edge between anticipation and satisfaction, fighting the orgasm she'd usually be reaching for with both hands.

"Pinch your nipples hard enough to hurt," Jackson ordered, his fingers replacing his tongue, thrusting in and out of her pussy, daring her to come. "Then concentrate on the pain. Concentrate on the pain and fight your way back from the edge until I tell you to let go."

"Yes, sir," she said, her words ending in a ragged gasp for breath as his mouth covered her sex and he sucked all of her into his mouth.

It was a foreign feeling, but an insanely hot one. She pinched her nipples so hard the sting made her jaw clench, but she still wasn't certain she'd be able to hold back for long. He was too good, too intense, so skilled at bringing a woman pleasure she could have come half a dozen times if he'd allowed it.

"Please," she begged, panting as she fought to keep from shattering. But it was so hard to resist succumbing to the deep rhythmic pulls as he suckled her clit into his wet heat even as his tongue undulated inside of her.

"Please, please, please." Her begging became a chant, a prayer for mercy he ignored until she was moaning and writhing on the floor, so close to the edge she felt like she was losing her mind.

Only when she was wild for him, teeth bared in a grimace and nipples bruised from her own abuse did he pull away from her pussy and order in a deep, resonant voice that rippled through her like the first seismic tremor of an earthquake. "Come, princess."

Instantly, she did. She came so hard she literally saw stars, holes in the night that flashed and blinked behind her closed eyes. She came like desert grass meeting a match, like a boulder crashing down a mountain flattening everything in its path. She came screaming and bucking into his mouth and clawing her fingers into the ground because she needed something to hold on to, something to keep her connected to the physical world as she was leveled by the most intense orgasm of her life.

It was epic, beautiful, and so damned intense she knew she'd been ruined for anything less than this highest of highs, the dizzying pinnacle of pleasure on the mountaintops above the clouds, a place she hadn't realized existed until Jackson had taken her there.

It took what felt like forever for her pleasure to be done with her. By the time she finally lay sated on the ground, catching her breath as she stared up at the slowly whirling ceiling fan and her overheated skin cooled, Jackson was on his back beside her.

"That was…" She shook her head, at a loss for words, but feeling like she had to try. "Revolutionary."

Jackson grunted, an amused sound that made her think she'd pleased him. "And the longer you wait, the better it gets."

Hannah's breath rushed out. "I can't imagine anything better."

"You don't have to," he said, his fingertips

brushing hers. "I've got enough imagination for the both of us."

Hannah kept her gaze on the ceiling, resisting the urge to turn to look at the man beside her. If she kept her gaze on the spinning fan and the underside of the thickly thatched roof, she could pretend that this was a tender moment with a captivating new lover, not a cease fire in some kind of twisted, erotic war.

As long as she didn't turn to see the darkness in Jackson's eyes, she could look forward to his feats of imagination, instead of fearing him the way she should. It wasn't healthy or sane, but pretending kept her from falling apart when Jackson stood and left the room a few minutes later, without so much as a goodbye.

But then goodbyes were for people, not prisoners, and she had a feeling a lapse in manners would be far from the worst thing that happened to her while she was under Jackson's control.

LILI VALENTE

88

CHAPTER NINE

Hannah

Hannah spent the rest of the next day alone in her room, trying to recover from the most intense sexual encounter of her life.

She paced from one side of the large space to another without remembering how she got from Point A to Point B. She stood staring out at the fruit trees, mesmerized by the scenes of the night before playing out in her head, and came back to herself to realize she'd lost over an hour and Eva was already setting her dinner tray down on the glass coffee table beside her.

If it weren't for the ache between her legs and the way her ass throbbed every time she sat down, it would have been easy to dismiss the entire encounter as a dream. Surely no man could make a woman feel the way Jackson had made her feel, especially not a woman he hated, whose mind he was determined to dismantle piece by piece.

But the more clues she gathered about the past, the easier it became to understand why he hungered for revenge.

She couldn't stop thinking about the things he'd let slip last night—about the police not being able to spot a real victim and the bruises Harley had faked—and piecing together how those things could combine to make a man so angry he would dedicate his life to tracking down the woman who had wronged him. Taking into account what she knew about her twin, it didn't take much imagination to guess that Harley had framed Jackson.

Framed him for something awful.

The bruises could have been part of an assault charge, but Hannah's gut said that wouldn't have been enough for Harley. When

Harley wanted to punish someone, she went for the jugular. She wanted her vengeance to hurt and to keep hurting for as long as possible.

And what would hurt a man like Jackson the most? A man who had been so crazy about Harley it whispered from his hands, lingered in every word, poured from his soul when he made love?

What would destroy a man who would have died before he laid a hand on his lover in anger?

By the time the sun sank behind the mountains at the rear of the property and birds began to fill the yard, feasting on the insects emerging into the cool dusk air, Hannah was certain that Harley had accused Jackson of rape and that at least a few people had believed her.

What she didn't know was why.

Why had Jackson become Harley's target in the first place? Based on Hannah's one night with him pre-private island, her gut instinct was that he was a good man—intense in the bedroom, but as tender-hearted as he was

Dominant. But now she knew that he had a dark side. A black as sin side. She had no doubt that he would destroy Aunt Sibyl in his quest for vengeance without thinking twice about it. She also had no doubt that he was a criminal and every bit as dangerous as Eva's son had said he was.

But what had come first? Was he a bad man who had earned Harley's twisted brand of justice? Or was it Harley's lies that had transformed a good man into a person ruled by hate and bitterness?

She didn't know, which was why she had to get permission to leave her room. She would never get to a cell phone or a computer if she was trapped in the master suite all day.

She told herself that's why she was so desperate to see Jackson again, but lying to herself was getting harder with every day she spent in captivity, forced to confront the truth in all its forms.

And the truth was that every cell in her body hungered for Jackson's touch. She longed for his hands on her breasts, his tongue in her mouth, his cock shoving into where she was already sore and aching.

She knew it would hurt to take him again so soon, but she wanted the pain. She wanted the pain and the pleasure and the closeness she'd felt in those few breathless minutes they'd lain side by side on the floor in the dark, their fingertips barely touching.

"What's wrong with you," she muttered as she finished her dinner and turned her teacup over, preparing to pour herself some of the chamomile tea Eva had taken to bringing to help her sleep. But underneath the cup, tucked neatly beneath the tea bag, she found a piece of paper folded into a tiny square.

Tea forgotten, Hannah unfolded the paper to reveal a few words scribbled hastily on the page:

I'm watching. Don't be afraid. I won't let him hurt you. Be strong and wait for my signal. I'll get to you before it's too late. —A friend

Crumpling the note in her fist, Hannah looked up, scanning the world outside her prison. Was this from Eva? From her son? Or was Adam, the pilot, not as obedient as he'd seemed during their flight to the island?

Or maybe this was from Hiro, the man she'd thought was a true friend before he'd helped facilitate her sale to a monster.

Whoever it was, she wasn't sure what they meant by a signal, but she would certainly be keeping an eye out for anything that looked remotely like a sign. It was comforting to know someone was concerned for her, but her less optimistic side insisted that getting away from Jackson wouldn't be so simple.

If there was a traitor in his midst, she had little doubt the man was already two steps ahead of the person who had offered to help her.

Just like he'll stay two steps ahead of you and make sure you never get to that computer to type his name into a search engine.

The thought was depressing, and her tea tasted pungently sweet in her mouth instead of comforting the way it had the night before.

She moved mechanically through her shower and headed to bed not long after dark, but she knew sleep was going to be hard to come by. Her skin felt too tight and every nerve in her body raw and agitated. She tossed and turned for over an hour, shifting from lying on her side, gaze fixed on the door, to flopping the other way to stare out at the patio.

She didn't know which point of entry Jackson had used the night before, but she wanted to see him coming if he joined her again tonight, to be alert and aware instead of waking up already wet and aching and half out of her mind with lust.

Outside, the moon was rising, casting the trees in peaceful blue light. She longed to step through the sliding glass door, to feel the grass cool on her bare feet and the breeze whispering across her feverish skin. It felt like years since she'd been outside and waiting for Jackson was making her feel her captivity even more keenly.

Finally, as midnight came and went and the clock crept closer toward one, she admitted that sleep was a lost cause. She was too on edge, too desperate for contact and the chance to get closer to solving the mystery of the man who owned her.

She flung off the covers, wrapped her toga

sheet around her breasts, and padded across the wooden floor. When she reached the glass, she couldn't resist sliding the door open and letting the wind in through the screen door. The villa was one of the few she'd encountered in the islands that had air conditioning, and it had been humming steadily during her entire visit, but Jackson hadn't said that she couldn't open the door. He'd just said that she couldn't leave the room or he would punish her.

The thought sent electricity coursing through her, like lightning dancing across water. It was a beautiful, dangerous feeling and before she knew what she was doing she was reaching for the screen door and sliding it open.

She was about to step one bare foot over the threshold and onto the concrete patio when a voice sounded from outside the door.

"I was wondering how long it would take for you to disobey me," he said, his voice as deep and delicious as it had been last night when he'd asked her if she wanted him to fuck her.

Against all common sense, Hannah smiled. "I haven't disobeyed you. I've only opened the door. I haven't left the room, sir."

"But you were about to," he said, shifting in the padded lounge chair he'd pulled up beside the door sometime between the time she'd gone to bed and when she'd finally given up hope of sleep.

In the soft moonlight, she could make out the outline of his features, but not his expression. She couldn't be sure if he was angry or in the mood to play, the way he had been last night after her spanking, but for some reason she sensed she wasn't in trouble. At least not yet.

But she could be…

She pointed her toe, letting it hover above the unblemished concrete as she circled her ankle. "What will you do if I step outside, sir?"

"Harley…"

Her sister's name was a warning, but she wasn't sure if she wanted to obey or not. To be a good girl or a bad one. It was hard to choose, when he made punishment feel so good.

"I broke a rule last night," he continued softly, his deep voice setting things to stirring inside of her, making her even more anxious for his touch.

"What rule was that?"

"I told myself I wasn't going to fuck you with my mouth," he said. "That it was too good for you. That you didn't deserve that type of pleasure from me."

Hannah brought her foot back to the floor inside, torn between indignation—she wasn't her sister, and she wasn't a foul thing unworthy of his kiss—and empathy. He wasn't the man she'd met that night six years ago and whether she'd had good reason or not, Harley was to blame.

Jackson was profoundly changed, but there was still a hint of vulnerability beneath his merciless exterior, and she wanted to get closer to that soft spot, not farther away. She wanted him to feel in control so that he would loosen the restraints he'd placed upon her and let her out of her cage.

But how could she make that happen when

he'd set so many rules for himself? Rules they seemed destined to break as the chemistry between them flared hotter with each encounter?

Finally, she decided she had no choice but to ask and hope he could hear the sincerity in her question.

"What can I do to make things better, sir?"

"Nothing," he murmured. "You have no power here, princess. Remember that. It is the only thing you need to remember."

"I understand," she said, curling her toes into the hardwood as knowing flickered to life in her bones.

It wasn't a thought so much as a feeling, a certainty that she should trust her instincts. She wasn't an experienced lover, let alone an experienced submissive, but her instincts hadn't led her astray last night. She'd pleased him and she could only hope that following that soft, sure voice inside her would please him again tonight.

"I know I have no power." She released her hold on the sheet, letting it fall to her feet, leaving her naked in the moonlight. "I'm here for your use." She waited until she felt his eyes on her in the near-darkness before she sank to her knees. "So use me, sir."

He shifted slightly in the chair. "Would you like that?"

"Yes, sir," she confessed, knowing she wouldn't be able to pull off a lie when her sex was already slick from the thought of his cock pushing between her lips.

"You'd like me to fuck your mouth?"

She dampened her lips, nerves tingling. "Yes, sir."

"Are you sure?" He rose from his seat, moving closer with that predatory gait of his. He was wearing dark pajama pants and no shirt, leaving his powerful chest and taut stomach bare to her gaze. He was as stunning as he was crazy and just a single look at him was enough to make her pussy wetter. "I won't be gentle. I won't stop when I hit the back of your throat. I'll fist my hand in your hair and force you to take it all, every inch."

She bit her lip, barely holding back a moan of arousal. "Yes, sir."

"I'll fuck you until tears run down your

cheeks and spit leaks from your chin." He stopped in front of her, reaching out to tangle his hand softly in her hair, making her ache to wrap her arms around his legs and rub against the silken fabric of his pajama pants like a cat desperate to be petted. "I will use you until you're jaw feels like it's about to snap in two and then I'll come so deep down your throat you'll have no choice but to swallow every drop."

She let her head fall back, not bothering to try to control the way her breasts rose and fell as her breath grew faster.

She wanted him to see what he did to her, how much she wanted everything he'd just described. She wanted him to take her mouth and then she wanted him to throw her on the bed and claim her body the way he had last night, soothing away the shame of the punishment with pleasure. She wanted his smile between her legs, his face twisting with passion as he labored above her, as lost in the magic they made as she was.

She knew there were no guarantees that she would see Jackson's patient, gentle side again, but it didn't matter. She would take his anger and punishment if that's all he would give her. She wanted him whatever way he would have her and she seemed to have no more control over that than the wind whipping through the trees outside, forcing the limber trunks to bend.

"Have you ever deep throated a cock before, Harley?"

"No, sir. But I want to try."

"It's going to hurt," he warned. "Especially the first time."

"I don't care," she whispered. "Please."

He made a soft, hungry sound low in his throat and his hand tightened into a fist in her hair, sending another shockwave of arousal coursing through her. "All right, princess. Then sit back on your heels and open wide."

She let her jaw drop and her tongue slip out to cover the edges of her bottom teeth, her body buzzing with awareness as he shoved his pajama pants lower on his hips, freeing his engorged length. Her nipples tightened as his cock bobbed free, seeming even larger from this angel, with the thick, turgid length pointing directly down toward her face.

Her eyes widened and worry that she would choke on him whispered through her, but before anxiety could become fear he guided his leaking head to her lips and pushed inside.

The salty, musky, Jackson taste of him washed over her tongue as he glided in slow, pausing as he neared the back of her throat to adjust the angle of her head with the fist still clenched in her hair. Hannah hummed around his thick head, relishing how soft the spongy flesh of his cock felt against her tongue.

"Relax your neck," he said, murmuring soft sounds of approval as she tilted her head farther back, relaxing into his control. "Good, now your shoulders. Let your shoulders fall away from your ears. That should relax your throat."

She obeyed and fresh saliva filled her mouth in response, easing the way for him to push deeper, slowly easing closer to the sensitive tissue that she feared would trigger her gag reflex.

She tensed instinctively, but he corrected her—

"Don't fight me. Relax. Relax your throat and as you feel yourself about to gag, swallow instead. Just swallow me down." He eased forward and she obeyed, slowly taking more of him, centimeter by centimeter of his massive length slipping down her throat while he whispered encouragement. "Yes, princess. Fuck, that's perfect. Don't worry about drooling. Your spit feels so fucking good on my cock."

She continued to work her mouth farther down his shaft, her breath coming faster as he kept going, sliding deep, deep down her throat.

"Breathe through your nose," he said, his hand gentling in her hair. "Don't panic. You can breathe. There's no reason to be afraid."

She moaned around his cock, wanting to tell him that she wasn't anxious, she was insanely turned on and dying for him to touch her, to pinch her nipples and slide his fingers into where she ached.

Yes, there was something scary about being

invaded by him in a way that felt so unnatural. But it was also empowering, to know that her mind was exerting control over her body and insisting that it accommodate her demands. *His* demands.

Right now, they felt like one and the same, and no matter how tough a game he'd talked leading up to this, he wasn't hurting her. He was coaching her, teaching her, the way he had last night. He was insistent, but patient, giving her time and only sliding in that last inch when she was wide open and ready to accept him.

They groaned in mutual pleasure as he sank home, his entire length buried inside her throat and the tip of her tongue resting against his balls. The taste of him flooded her mouth and his scent spun through her head. He smelled like soap and spice and man. *The* man, the one she'd been waiting for, the man whose taste was the best taste and smell was the best smell. The man whose soul hummed at the same frequency as her own and whose touch made her feel safe, even when he was rough with her.

Especially then. She had never felt freer than when Jackson loomed so large in her awareness that there was no room for anything or anyone else.

As he fisted his hand in her hair, sliding out and back in, slowly establishing a rhythm, giving her time to adjust to the way he glided up and down her tongue, she let go of everything. She let go of worry and doubt. She let go of her hopes and fears and plans for coaxing a way out of her cage.

She let go of herself and became nothing but the woman kneeling at Jackson's feet, the source of his pleasure, the goddess who made his breath hitch and this strong, complicated, troubled man come undone. And instead of that giving away making her less, it made her more.

She felt powerful, beautiful, and unashamed of the saliva dripping down her chin as his thrusts grew faster, deeper. The mess was part of the pleasure, and that made it beautiful too.

A beautiful mess.

Like her, like Jackson, and whatever this

was growing between them.

She rolled her eyes up to watch his face. Her sight had adjusted to the shadows enough that she could make out his full bottom lip trapped between his teeth and the way his hard features relaxed as he neared the edge. And in that moment he was her stranger again, the one she'd promised herself to the first time he'd taken her in his arms.

He was vulnerable and overcome and as devastated by what was happening between them as she was. It was enough to make her hope again, but then he thrust forward one last time with a groan, his cock jerking deep in her throat, and once again there was nothing but him.

Nothing but the way he owned her every time they touched.

CHAPTER TEN

Jackson

Jackson came like a steam engine roaring off the tracks, like lava bursting from the center of the earth. His entire body exploded with bliss, not just his pulsing cock or throbbing balls.

He came in his legs and his arms and deep in his chest where his heart swelled to push against the bones that caged it. He came in the fingertips buried in the silken softness of her hair. He came in the lips that buzzed with blood and heat and the longing to replace his cock with his mouth and kiss Harley breathless.

Kiss her until she moaned and begged and confessed every thought racing through her head. Until she laid her secrets bare and finally told him the truth about something other than how much she wanted him to fuck her.

Before he could bring himself to care about breaking another one of his stupid rules, he was pulling his spent cock from between Harley's lips and lifting her up by the hand he'd fisted in her hair.

She moaned as she rose to her feet and fell into him, her arms twining around his neck and her breasts flattening against his chest. Her lips parted and he bent his head, crushing his mouth to hers, pushing his tongue into her heat, tasting sex and submission.

And it was sweet. And filthy. And fucking perfect.

Her tongue sparred with his, giving as good as she got as he pulled her in tight with one arm, drawing her up his body, needing to get closer to her wicked mouth. They kissed like they needed the other's lips to survive, like they were the last refugees of some terrible war.

And Jackson supposed, in a way, they were. Harley had started the war and he would finish it. She had ruined him and he planned to wreck her in return and maybe by the end of it all no one would understand either of them the way they understood each other. They would be broken in the same way, twisted mirror reflections.

He kissed her until his spent cock began to swell between his legs and Harley was making eager little mewling sounds before he finally set her on her feet and pulled back to look into her shadowed face.

"Good, sir?" she asked, swaying slightly, her voice husky and ripe with lust.

"You're a deep throat prodigy," he said, wiping the wetness on her chin away with one hand. "Now put your hands behind your back and interlace your fingers."

She obeyed immediately, her movements bringing her breasts into tighter contact with his feverish skin. Even with the breeze rushing in from the ocean, he was burning up, already dying to have her again not five minutes after he'd come like it was the last, best thing he would ever do.

"You did so well," he said, cupping her breasts in his hands and capturing her swollen tips between his fingers and thumbs. "So I'm going to give you a choice between two rewards."

She held his gaze, breath coming faster as he plucked and teased her nipples. "Thank you, sir."

"The first reward is an afternoon on the beach tomorrow, all by yourself," he said, cock thickening as she smiled and arched into his touch. "The second is an afternoon spent exploring the island with me, followed by dinner together tomorrow night."

"The second," she said, thighs shifting. "With you, sir."

"Are you sure?" he asked. "I don't promise to be nice to you or give a shit if you have a good time."

"With you, sir," she repeated a pained look flashing across her face. "Please, can I touch you? I want to touch you."

"Why?" He dropped one hand between her

legs, sliding a finger through her slick folds. She was already dripping, and clearly hadn't been faking her enjoyment in having his cock rammed down her throat.

"I want to get closer to you," she said, moaning as he began to circle her swollen clit. "I want to dig my fingernails into your shoulders while you fuck me."

"But I'm in charge of pain." He leaned down, kissing her cheek before leaning in to whisper into her ear. "And who said I was going to fuck you?"

"You can't blame a girl for wishful thinking. Especially when you've got your hand between her legs," she said, trapping his ear lobe between her teeth and biting down.

"Good point," he said, plunging a finger between her legs, making her gasp and her mouth open. "But your reward doesn't start until tomorrow afternoon. There's still plenty of time to make you suffer." He pinched her nipple, drawing a moan from low in her throat.

Her head fell back. "I know, sir."

"So what if I said I was leaving you now,"

he said, the mere thought enough to make his balls ache with grief. "And that you were to go to bed without doing anything to bring yourself relief?"

"That's what I would do," she said, even as she widened her stance, making it easier for him to add a second finger and push deeper inside her. "I don't want my own hand. I want your cock."

"You want my cock, sir," he corrected, though his cock couldn't care less if she added the honorific. His cock just wanted inside her, five minutes ago.

"I want your cock, sir," she amended, her eyes so filled with hunger he wasn't sure he would be able to deny her, even in the name of making her suffer. "I want to be so full of you there's no room for anything else."

"You're a tremendous liar, Harley." His pulse raced as he added a third finger and rammed in deep, making her breath catch. "A fucking master of the art."

"Nothing I've said tonight has been a lie," she said, holding his gaze. "Not a thing. I want you. I've wanted you from the first moment I saw you. You drive me crazy, Jackson, and I—"

He silenced her with another bruising kiss. He couldn't let her keep talking or he'd slap her. Or shake her until her teeth rattled. Or pin her to the wall and howl into her face until she stopped fucking with him and told him why.

Why she did it, why she cheated on him, why she ran away with Clay, why she framed him for a crime he didn't commit, a crime he never would have committed because he was a good man.

Or he had been a good man. Then.

He wasn't now, and she would do well to remember it.

"You will not use my given name again," he growled against her lips as he picked her up with one arm and carried her toward the bed where the bedside lamp cast the rumpled covers in soft yellow light. "Or I will hurt you. And it will not be the kind of hurting you enjoy."

"Yes, sir," she breathed. "I'm sorry, sir."

"Shut up." He threw her onto the bed,

where she landed with a yip of surprise that would have made him laugh once, back when he'd loved all her little sounds. Now it just made his jaw clench. "Hands above your head, pinned to the bed. Do not move them from that position or I will stop whatever I'm doing immediately and leave the room."

She scooted backward, watching him warily as she lay down and lifted her hands above her head. "I'm sorry, sir."

"You've said that, but now I want you to be quiet," he said, shoving his pants to the ground and stepping out of them. "I don't want you to make a sound. Not a moan, not a whimper, not a single sound. Do you understand?"

She nodded, eyes widening as he wrapped his hands around her ankles and squeezed.

"Not even when you come," he warned. "If you cry out when you come it will be the last time you come for days and that's a promise."

She pressed her lips together and nodded again.

"Good. Now let's see how you're doing

after last night." He pushed her legs up and over her head, until her knees touched her nose and her ass was up in the air. She was as flexible as ever and it was fucking hot, but not as hot as the faint red and blue marks covering her pale buttocks.

He ran a hand over them, gently kneading the flesh. She cringed slightly, but didn't whimper. Either he wasn't using enough force to hurt her or she was simply determined not to make a sound.

One way to find out…

He slapped her ass hard enough to set her flesh to jiggling and definitely hard enough to hurt the parts of her that were already bruised. But still she was silent.

He glanced down between her legs to see her eyes closed and her teeth digging in to her bottom lip. She was so obedient when she wanted to be, so eager to be led, so seemingly effortlessly submissive. If he didn't know better, it would be easy to believe this was the truth and everything else had been the lie. Even his gut was sold. It believed she wanted him and needed this sick game they were playing as much as he did.

But he'd spent eighteen months behind bars for the mistake of believing in Harley Garrett—or whatever the hell her name was—and he wasn't going to make that mistake again. She had always been strong enough not to get swept up in her own deception. Now it was his turn to prove he was her equal.

He would keep pushing until she broke. Sooner or later he'd find her limit, the line she wasn't willing to cross in the name of pretending to be what he wanted and then he would see the woman behind the mask. He would force the real Harley from hiding and then force her to her knees, no matter how long it took.

He'd promised to return her in a month, but she knew better than most that promises were made to be broken.

The thought made his cock thicker and the need to be balls deep in Harley more powerful. Hating her made him want to fuck her as much as love ever had, proving there was indeed a thin line between one and the other.

Holding her legs above her head with one hand looped around both of her ankles, Jackson reached for the box of condoms she'd left on top of the table with the other. The decision had no doubt been a calculated move, one of her many attempts to prove herself willing and eager to please. Like choosing an afternoon with him instead of an afternoon alone on the beach.

But she would regret that decision, sooner or later. Every moment she spent with him was taking her a step closer to her own destruction.

Let her think otherwise. For now. Let her think about the pleasure he gave her and the small kindnesses he showed her and let her think he was weakening. It didn't matter what she thought; nothing had changed and nothing would ever change. No matter how many times she made him come, no matter how she excelled at getting him off, he would never soften or sway. He would stay on course until he was running her over, leaving bits and pieces of her shattered soul littering the road behind him.

Breath coming faster, he ripped the condom open with his teeth and slid it on his pulsing length before returning both hands to Harley's ankles and pushing her legs even farther back, until her face was framed by her muscled calves.

"Look at me," he ordered.

She opened her eyes, worry and lust mixing in the blue depths.

"You said you wanted to be so full of me there was no room for anything else," he said as he brought the head of his cock to her opening and applied the barest teasing pressure. "In this position you will feel every inch. You're going to feel me in your ribs. You're going to feel me in your throat, where you're still sore from taking me there."

She swallowed, but the worry faded from her expression and her tongue slipped out to dampen her lips.

"Does that excite you?"

Her eyes darkened as she nodded.

"It's going to hurt at first," he warned, pushing a little deeper, until the head of his cock eased inside her.

She shook her head slowly side to side.

"It will," he assured her, as excited by the anticipation of the first deep thrust as by her slick cunt gripping the tip of him. "I don't plan on going slow. I'm going to take what's mine."

Holding his gaze, she silently mouthed, "Then take it, sir," and he had no choice but to give her what she'd asked for.

He dropped his hips, plunging inside her gripping sheath with a groan. Even when she was this turned on—dripping and slick for him—they were a tight fit. Her body fought him, unable to adjust to his girth so quickly. He knew it hurt her, could see it in the way she grimaced as he kept pushing, forcing her to take every inch, until his balls were snug against her ass and his head rammed into her cervix.

But by the time he thrust deep a third time, she was bucking into him, eager to be fucked harder, deeper, and he was happy to oblige. He rode her like he hated her—pounding her pussy until he knew she would be even more bruised—and relished the way her slick sheath nearly snapped him in two with the force of her release like he loved her. He hated the way she smiled through the pain he inflicted and loved the way she remained utterly silent as she came a second time, milking his cock into the most intense orgasm of his life.

He came so hard the world vanished, and there was nothing but throbbing bliss and pleasure and the harmony of two bodies that fit together so perfectly.

Twisted and misshapen and perverse, but perfect.

She destroyed him and lifted him up to heights no man could reach alone. And he loved it and hated it and loathed himself for his weakness even as he flipped her over and began to take her again, claiming her from behind until his flaccid cock became hard and he'd fucked a third and fourth orgasm from Harley's dripping cunt and refilled the condom with another gush of pain and pleasure.

Love and hate.

Him and her.

And it was terrible. And wonderful. And by the time he'd worn her out and tucked her limp body beneath the covers he knew it was time to take the next step. He was weakening, but so was she.

Now it was time to push her over the edge, and to show her there would be a price to pay for refusing to fall.

CHAPTER ELEVEN

Hannah

Hannah spent the rest of the night in the grips of the worst nightmare she'd had in years. It was one of those un-put-down-able nightmares that sent her surging awake with her heart in her throat only to pick up where it left off as soon as she managed to fall back to sleep.

In the dream, she was one of the Carolina Cult Girls, five young women who had been kidnapped from their homes when they were barely teens and forced to marry into a Doomsday cult deep in the Smoky Mountains.

They'd been held captive for years before they were found and were all the news stations could talk about the spring of Hannah's senior year of college.

As a leader in the fields of both child psychology and PTSD, Dr. Patricia Connolly, Hannah's mentor at Duke, had worked extensively with two of the young women after their rescue. Hannah had tagged along to the sessions to take notes, honored by the chance to observe her professor in action and to get an insider's perspective on such a troubling case. She had hoped it would help her in her own practice later in life, but she'd left each session more disturbed than the last.

The first girl, Mary Ellen, was eighteen at the time of her rescue and had two young children by her much older husband. She'd been the youngest of his five wives and according to her account had been treated like a princess during her captivity. Her husband was an elder in their church, well off in the world of the cult, and besotted with the pretty new addition to his family.

But the moment Mary Ellen was set free,

she placed her children in the custody of the state, got a makeover, changed her name, and did everything she could to put her six years of captivity behind her. Despite her best efforts, she was plagued by anxiety and so terrified of losing her autonomy a second time that she lashed out at anyone she perceived as an authority figure, including her therapist. Once, Hannah had been forced to help pin the slim woman to the floor to keep her from attacking Dr. Connolly with a letter opener she'd snatched from the desk.

Three months into her therapy, Mary had started drinking to excess to self-medicate her anxiety. Not long after, she disappeared again, leaving her family even more heartbroken than they'd been before.

They had been so overjoyed to have Mary back, but the girl they remembered didn't exist anymore. She had been broken into a thousand pieces and no one—not even one of the best psychiatrists in the country—was able to put her back together again.

Ella Small, the second young woman, was thirteen when she was taken and sixteen when she was rescued. She'd spent half the time in the cult that Mary had, had no children, and had been married to a younger, less powerful cult member with seven wives and not enough money to feed them all. She'd gone hungry, had a miscarriage brought about by a beating from her sister-wives, and her relationship with her husband had been strained to say the least.

During her sessions she recalled that he would often be kind and understanding about her bigger failings, only to turn around and beat her and lock her in the stocks for public shaming when she forgot to coop the chickens for the night or left the butter out.

But instead of being even more eager than her counterpart to return to a normal life, Ella Small longed for the compound and regretted that she had no children by her cult husband to "remember him by" now that he was going to prison for the rest of his life. She admitted that she didn't love him, but expressed regret that she hadn't been able to make the marriage more successful—the marriage she'd been forced into after being kidnapped from a playground during her little brother's softball game.

Hannah's professor had found Ella's case to be a classic example of Stockholm Syndrome, a form of capture-bonding in which the victim empathizes with and becomes emotionally attached to their tormentor. Dr. Connolly said Ella had subconsciously identified with her abusive husband as a way of protecting herself from the harmful psychological effects of prolonged captivity.

Before those eerie sessions, Hannah had understood Stockholm Syndrome, but only in a textbook way. Coming face to face with an innocent young girl who had been stolen from a loving home, raped for the first months of her "marriage," and forced to live a nightmare for years—but who seemed unable to wake up from the false belief that her cult husband was a decent man who tried his best to provide—was more chilling than she'd expected it to be.

It brought home in a new way the immense power of the human mind.

The mind was innovative, beautiful, and endlessly creative, but it could also be terrifying. Ella's body had been liberated from her prison, but her mind was still locked away, trapped in a dangerous pattern of thinking that allowed the man who had stolen her youth to continue stealing from her long after he was behind bars.

For months after those sessions, Hannah had suffered from horrible nightmares. In her dreams, she'd been working as a therapist, but was unable to get through to the children who had come to her for help. The children were the saddest of sad cases, innocents who had been violently victimized and bore mental and emotional scars that tore her heart in two. She would wake up covered in a cold sweat, her pulse racing, consumed by the fear that she might not be up to the challenge of freeing her future patients from the unhealthy machinations of their own minds.

But when Jackson left her alone in bed— disappearing as soon as he thought she was asleep—Hannah didn't have one of her therapist anxiety dreams. She dreamed that she was one of those lost girls.

She was a teenager trapped in the same shack where Ella had shared a single bedroom with six other women, waiting for her husband to come home. She cooked fried chicken in the nude while her sister-wives watched and laughed when the hot oil leapt out of the skillet to scald her skin.

Later, she waited for her husband on her knees by the door and allowed him to take her on the filthy carpet as soon as he stepped inside. His touch made her sick to her stomach, but she parted her legs and endured it because she knew she had no choice but to obey.

And then the dream skipped ahead and she was pregnant with the man's child and happy, feeding chickens in a threadbare dress not adequate to protect her from the crisp autumn air, daydreaming about how wonderful things were going to be now that the baby was coming. Some part of her mind was horrified by the shift in her thinking, but that part was growing weaker and more distant with every passing day.

Soon, she wouldn't be able to hear it at all.

One morning, she would wake up and no longer see that she was being tortured, degraded, and abused. And on that day she would be as much a captive of her own mind as of the man who had taken her away from the people who loved her.

Hannah moaned as she sat up in bed, rubbing at the tops of her aching eyes with her fingertips, shivering as she tried to shake off the lingering emotional fog the dream had left behind. She couldn't remember the last time a nightmare had made her physically ill, but right now it was all she could do not to race to the bathroom and be sick.

It had been so real, so horribly real.

Because it is real. The setting is prettier, but the scenario is the same.

You've been taken by a dangerous man, isolated, put under his control, and sooner or later you will bend or you will break.

"No," Hannah mumbled softly to herself, hugging her knees to her chest. She wouldn't end up like Mary or Ella. She wasn't an impressionable, terrified young girl. She was a strong, intelligent woman capable of doing what it took to survive without breaking down or falling under Jackson's dark spell.

She refused to think about how close she'd felt to him last night or how much it had hurt when he'd lashed out and refused to let her say his name.

Last night was last night. She'd been exhausted, vulnerable, and lonely. This morning she was going to keep her eye on the prize—an entire afternoon outside of this damned room—and get her head back in the right place.

An afternoon in the sun would surely help with that. It seemed like she'd been in this cage forever, with nothing but memories of her intense erotic encounters with Jackson to keep her company. A taste of normalcy was all she needed to remember that this would be over soon and she would be back to being Hannah again, with none of her sister's demons haunting her days or owning her nights.

And there was a friend out there

somewhere. She couldn't forget that.

Someone on this island was watching out for her and determined to save her before it was too late. Jackson cast a large shadow in her mind, but no man was infallible and there was a chance that her secret friend would escape his notice. She clung to that hope as she made the bed and headed into the bathroom to wash the smell of her tormentor/lover from her skin.

Hannah showered and braided her hair in a loose French braid that trailed half way down her back. She didn't know what Jackson had planned for them, but it was windy outside and she couldn't stand the feel of hair flying into her face. Since moving to the island, her hair practically lived in a ponytail.

She'd been tempted once or twice to cut it short and let it whip into a froth of wild curls atop her head like Eloise, who worked at the sandwich shop in town, but she'd never had a haircut different from her sister's. From the time they were little, Harley had always insisted they cut their hair the same way and Hannah had bowed to her sister's preference for long hair with several tiered layers.

She had a habit of bowing.

The more she thought about her life and her choices, the more clear it became that she had a strong natural inclination toward the kind of sexual relationship Jackson enjoyed. She had always bowed to the more powerful personalities in her life. It made her happier to be of service than to get her own way. She wasn't a doormat and stood up for herself when necessary, but submitting to someone she cared about made her feel useful, productive, and content.

Focusing on someone else's needs aside from her own made her feel safe. To be of service, and to have that service appreciated, *was* her need, and the primary driving force of her personality. But she wanted to serve someone who cared about her and respected her, someone she could trust not to take advantage of her generous spirit.

No matter how much she'd loved Harley, her sister had never been that sort of person. She had abused Hannah's trust and forgiving heart and, if Harley had lived, Hannah knew

LILI VALENTE

that they would have eventually come to a crossroads. Either Harley would have had to change the way she did business, or Hannah would have been forced to withdraw from their relationship, no matter how painful that would have been.

Jackson was a lot like her sister, so focused on his own needs that he didn't care about the destruction he left in his wake. She had no choice but to submit to him physically and to let him see how much she enjoyed it, but she had a choice about how far her submission went. She had to keep her heart tightly locked away. There was no room for empathy or hurt feelings where Jackson was concerned. If she let herself get any closer to him than she felt already she might very well end up like Ella, locked in a mental prison of her own making.

"You have to stay strong," she whispered to her reflection. "No matter what Harley did to him, it doesn't make it okay for him to hurt you. Whatever happens today, remember that. If he punishes you for something you didn't do, it's okay to enjoy it, but it's not okay to think you deserve it."

She took a deep breath, meeting her own haunted eyes in the mirror and wishing she looked as strong as she sounded. With a final deep breath and a silent promise to keep repeating her new mantra for as long as it took for it to stick, she wrapped up in a towel and stepped out of the bathroom to find her favorite breakfast—croissants and fresh fruit—waiting on the coffee table.

Even more exciting, however, were the new clothes spread out on the foot of the bed.

At the sight of the khaki cargo shorts and black tank top—with a built in bra, thank God, she was so sick of going without one— her heart flipped over and a giddy grin broke out across her face.

Clothes! Real clothes!

She practically skipped across the room, squealing with delight when she saw the socks and hiking boots on the floor on the other side of the bed.

She was going outside and it looked like Jackson had something active planned! She was so thrilled. After days of stagnantly stewing she was dying for a long hike through the jungle, or up to the bluffs above the sea. Any place where she could breathe deep and feel the eternal, peaceful pulse of nature whispering across her skin.

Where she could feel her blood rush and her skin heat for reasons that had nothing to do with sex or the man who was quickly becoming the seductive black hole at the center of her universe.

She dressed quickly, hands shaking with happiness as she covered her nakedness, even putting the socks and shoes on, though she never wore shoes in the house at home. But if felt so good to have something to wear, to be granted that small privilege. When she was through, she wrapped her arms around herself and held on tight, relishing the way the cotton and spandex of the tank top clung to her skin, helping hold her weakening center together.

If Jackson were here right now, she would throw herself into his arms and hug him until he grunted. She wouldn't be able to help herself. She was just so grateful.

Grateful for clothing, giddy because he's stopped forcing you to walk around in nothing but a sheet, feeling vulnerable and exposed.

Hannah's smile faded and the happy butterflies in her belly died a quick death, falling to the floor of her stomach where they began to fester and rot.

The voice of reason was right. She could enjoy these clothes, but she shouldn't be grateful for them. Jackson didn't deserve credit for easing up on a punishment or for pleasure delivered on his terms. She couldn't afford to start feeling gratitude for anything Jackson gave her except her freedom at the end of this month and the full payment of her promised fee.

With that thought firmly in mind, she sat down to eat her breakfast, determined to keep her head in the right place and make the most of her afternoon of freedom.

CHAPTER TWELVE

Jackson

Jackson asked the cook to prepare a picnic lunch and then deliberately added the cooler pouch with three water bottles and two fruit juices into Harley's pack, simply to add a little extra pain to what promised to be a miserable experience.

For Harley, anyway.

She'd seemed to enjoy their strolls on the beach years ago, but she'd clearly been miserable the one time he'd taken her hiking on his favorite stretch of the Appalachian trail a few weeks before she'd disappeared. She'd complained for most of the six-mile hike and acted like the small camelback water pack he'd brought for her weighed a hundred pounds.

That was the first time Jackson had realized how out of shape she was. Back then Harley had been slim—almost too skinny for his tastes—but she'd maintained her weight by watching what she ate, not exercise. By the end of the trail, he'd been beating himself up for taking her on such a grueling hike. They should have started out slow, to build up her endurance.

Now, he was looking forward to watching her attempt to maintain her "I live to serve" attitude while being forced to hike five miles up hill through a close, humid rainforest and then five miles back down again. By the time they were back at the trailhead, he expected her to be reaching the end of her rope. It would then be a simple business to snip the last few threads tethering her to her self-control and watch her submissive façade melt away.

It was time to force the real Harley out of hiding, before he became any more addicted to the excellent performance she'd been giving in the bedroom. That was another lie, and by tonight he would have the proof snarling and spitting in his face as they embarked on the second phase of their perverse new relationship.

The thought made him smile as he knocked on Harley's door.

A moment later she appeared, flinging open the door with an eager grin on her face, looking refreshed and lovely in the simple clothes he'd had Adam purchase yesterday when the pilot went to the nearest island with a large grocery store and hardware store for supplies.

"Hello again." Her gaze flicked up and down his body and a soft laugh escaped her lips. "You look different in shorts."

He arched one brow. "How so?"

"I don't know," she said, shaking her head. "Less scary, I guess."

"Well, I assure you, I'm still every bit as scary," he said, though he couldn't seem to force the usual gruffness into his tone. He was looking forward to watching Harley's sunny disposition wither too much to channel the full power of his rage today. "And I've got a terrifying afternoon planned for you. Are you ready to go?"

She looked up at him, eyes wide and curious as she searched his features. But apparently whatever she found in his expression wasn't any scarier than his khaki cargo shorts because she smiled again. "You're joking, right? There's nothing terrifying on these islands except the centipedes."

"You'll see," he said, nodding his head. "Follow me. We'll pick up our packs in the kitchen and leave through the garden door."

"All right," she said, practically skipping through the door to follow him down the hall, and into the kitchen. "It's a beautiful day."

"It is," he said, nodding at the cook as he passed Harley the blue backpack and took the black for himself. Black, like his soul, and Harley was a fool to forget that even for a moment.

"Hello, Eva," she chirped to the cook who nodded nervously before retreating to the other side of the kitchen to continue chopping vegetables. "Lots of water. Thank you so much." Harley continued, poking into her pack, seemingly unperturbed by the other woman's less-than-warm response. "Did you remember to pack sunscreen, Hawke? The sun on the islands is intense, even this time of year, and you don't have the base tan I have. You'll get burned faster than you think."

"I have sunscreen," he said, amused by her feigned concern. "But the first part of the trail is in the shade. We shouldn't need it until later."

Harley nodded, not missing a beat as she slung her pack on her back and bounced lightly on her toes. "All right. I'm ready whenever you are."

Her grin was a thing of beauty he couldn't wait to see shrivel as soon as she realized this was no stroll along the beach he had planned, but a grueling ten mile round-trip hike up and down the side of a mountain. Considering she was probably in worse shape now than she'd been six years ago, they would be lucky to make it back to the property before sundown.

But he'd brought a flashlight, too. He was prepared and every bit as eager as Harley to start their day.

"After you." He opened the door for her and followed her out into the sunny afternoon. "The trail head is at the back of the property. On the other side of the orange grove."

Harley sucked in a deep breath and titled her face to the sun as they crossed the wide lawn. "Thank you for this."

"You're welcome," he said, unable to keep from admiring how beautiful she was with the sun catching the red in her dark braid and a look of such naked pleasure on her face. "I hope you'll still be thanking me by the time we get back to the house for dinner."

She shot him a sideways glance. "Me, too." She bit her lip, but continued after a moment, "I hope it's alright that I haven't been calling you sir. I figured that was only for the bedroom, but…"

"It's fine," he said. "But my given name is still off limits. First names are for equals and that's not something we'll ever be."

"Of course." She nodded and her shoulders wilted, but after a moment her spirits seemed to lift again. As they circled around a fat palm and made their way through the rows of orange trees, the spring returned to her step. But then he supposed it was hard to take anything too seriously on an afternoon like this one, even revenge or captivity.

The smell of flowers and salt water mingled in the air and the sea breeze kept the cloudless day from feeling too warm. The garden was humming with life and exploding with color and when they reached the trailhead the forest seemed to welcome them in with open arms. The feathery leaves of the eucalyptus trees shielded them from the sun and the cool mud beneath their feet smelled pleasantly of earth and the spicy, fermenting scent of plants breaking down to become part of the soil.

For the first half-mile, Jackson shot regular glances Harley's way, waiting for her peaceful expression to grow strained. But by the time they started up the first incline—a slow but steady gain up the mountainside that granted peek-a-boo glimpses of the waves crashing on the shore below—he was getting lost in the comforting rhythm of one foot in front of the other.

Whether it was jogging in formation during training drills in the Marines or his daily run each morning, Jackson's mind was never more at peace than at moments like these, when the motion of the body became a soothing meditation, a way to rise above the demons that haunted him. Even before Harley, there had been darkness in his life and a deep surety that he would never feel at home in the world. His father had been a cold, merciless man and his mother far more concerned with her position in society than her husband or only son.

Neither of his parents seemed to consider love or emotion a valuable part of human life. From a young age, Jackson had been plagued by the certainty that there was something deeply flawed within him. He felt too much, too deeply, too often.

He'd been shattered when his dog Petra died when he was seven, so grief-stricken his mother had ordered him to stay in his room until he could stop disturbing the peace with his wailing. He'd spent nearly a week in his room, missing school and having his meals brought to him on a tray by the housekeeper, learning the hard lesson that he'd better keep his pain to himself if he expected to be allowed contact with the outside world.

There had been other hard lessons learned throughout the years, but none as cruel and final as the one Harley had taught him. She had cured him of his fatal flaw, his over-abundance of heart.

If his father could see the cold bastard he was today, he would be pleased.

He will *be pleased, when you deliver Harley to his front door and she confesses the truth.*

And then you will tell Ian Hawke to go fuck himself and prove just how well you've learned your lessons.

Usually thoughts of that final confrontation with his father would send the storm clouds rushing in to darken his thoughts, but the steady sound of his footfalls and the soothing in and out of his breath as the trail grew steeper kept him grounded. His savage beast was so soothed by the walk through the jungle and the stunning view that he and Harley had reached the second mile marker before he regained the presence of mind to realize his companion wasn't complaining.

In fact, she seemed as Zenned out by the hike as he was. Sweat dampened her hairline and beaded between her breasts, but her lips were curved in an absent-minded smile and her breath remained strong and even. And when they stopped at a lookout to soak in the increasingly dramatic view of the sea, she threw her arms open and sighed happily as if she were embracing the world and everything in it.

"Enjoying yourself?" Jackson asked, irritation creeping in to disturb his calm as he reached into Harley's pack for a bottle of water.

"Immensely," she chirped. "Incredibly immensely."

"You're in better shape than you used to be."

"Thanks. I try to hike or swim every day at home," she said, grinning up at him as he took a drink of the cool water. "It helps clear my head."

Wonderful, Jackson thought sourly, but his tone was carefully neutral when he said, "So you've discovered a love of exercise as well as an appreciation for food since we saw each other last."

Harley's happy expression fell, her brows furrowing as she crossed her arms at her chest. "If that's a crack about the weight I've gained, I don't appreciate it. I had enough of starving myself during high school and college. I'm healthy, happy the way I am, and it's ridiculous to think a woman only deserves to feel beautiful if she's a size zero."

"I agree," he said, not willing to stoop to petty insults in his quest to break her. "I like you better this way. Your body is stunning."

She blinked in surprise, her frown giving way to a pink flush that spread across her cheeks. "Well...thank you. I, um..." She glanced down at her feet as she tucked her hands into the back pockets of her shorts. "I don't know how to act when you're being nice."

"I'm not being nice, I'm being truthful," he said, but her words did give him something to think about. She could be faking this awkward moment, but he didn't think so. It seemed like she really was caught off guard by his honesty. And if that was the case, this day might not have to end in failure after all, not if he had the courage to tell the whole truth and nothing but the truth.

"All right," she said, lifting uncertain eyes to meet his. "Then I appreciate your honesty."

He nodded before holding the half empty water bottle up between them. "A drink before we continue? It's another three miles to the top."

"Yes. Thank you." She took the bottle hesitantly, holding his gaze as she took several long swallows.

The way her throat worked as she drank was sexy as hell and part of him wanted nothing more than to tug her shorts down around her ankles and have her against the nearest tree. To show her just how much he appreciated all the tempting new curves she'd developed.

But sex wasn't part of today's agenda. Not in his original plan and not in this new direction he had decided to take. He couldn't afford to have his focus clouded by the increasingly explosive chemistry between them.

Sex had served its purpose. Her defenses were weakening. He could read it in the glances she cast his way as they started up the mountain, feel it in the way she swayed closer to his side than she had during the first leg of their journey.

It made him wonder if she'd truly been faking her feelings for him all those years ago. Maybe she had felt something, but it simply hadn't been strong enough to compete with her driving need to destroy him. Maybe love and hate could co-exist within the same body at the same moment.

But hate would always win out in the end. He knew that the way he knew that the sun would set behind the mountain tonight and that Harley would end her day much less happily than she'd begun it.

CHAPTER THIRTEEN

Hannah

Something was changing between her and Jackson.

Hannah wasn't sure what it was, only that the air seemed easier to breathe after their talk at the lookout. The anger that had been his constant companion since they arrived on the island seemed to drift away in the sweet breeze threading through the trees and the silence that fell between them became a shared thing, not a door slammed in her face.

When she cast furtive glances his way, she

found his features soft and relaxed. He looked younger, freer than he had since the moment he removed her blindfold, and so beautiful it was enough to break her heart. *This* was the man she remembered, a man whose sharply angled face and dark eyes were softened by intelligence and thoughtfulness, a man who could be scary but never would be because he knew right from wrong.

She knew it was lunacy to believe a shared love of relaxing walks through the woods and her newer, fuller figure had changed Jackson's plans or her fate. But her gut practically sang with assuredness that something was different and things were going to be better between her and Jackson from here on out. He'd seen something in her, something that he could respect mingled in with all the things he hated.

It didn't mean the hard times were over, but it was a start, enough to make her wish this hike would last forever and they never had to go back to the warped world of the bedroom at the end of the hall.

Liar. You like that world and everything he's done to you in it.

Hannah wrinkled her nose. It was true, she did like what she and Jackson did together in bed, but it would be nice to know that when the games were over she could spend the rest of the night with this man, a person who didn't seem to resent the fact that she was allowed to draw breath.

They reached the summit at a little after two o'clock and spread out the picnic Eva had packed for them on a large flat rock, staring out at the jagged edge of the coastline far below as they unwrapped their toasted cheese, basil, and tomato sandwiches.

"It's nice not to have to worry about snakes, isn't it?" Hannah said, watching Jackson's powerful jaw work as he took his first bite, finding it fascinating to see him doing something as normal as eating a sandwich.

Maybe the man was human, after all.

"When we first moved to the islands," she continued, "I was always worried about running into snakes sunning themselves on rocks, until I learned there aren't any snakes here. Or poisonous spiders."

Jackson reached into his pack, pulling out a container filled with freshly cut vegetables and some sort of dip in a separate compartment. "So I'm the only predator you have to worry about up here, then?"

"I guess so," she said, the teasing note in his voice making it clear he was kidding. Besides, she wouldn't mind being preyed upon right now. It had been far too long since she'd felt his hands on her, and she was curious to learn if this new, easier feeling between them would follow them into the bedroom.

Curious, and a little anxious.

If fear were eliminated from the equation when they were skin to skin, it would be all too easy for another powerful emotion to sweep in and take its place. But she knew better than to think that any affection she felt for Jackson would ever be returned. He would never care about her and anything she imagined she felt for him was the result of a psychiatric disorder.

Better to keep him talking and enjoy the respite from their kinky sexual games as long as possible.

"Can I ask you a question?" she asked, shifting to face him instead of the stunning view. But Jackson was every bit as captivating, especially when he met her gaze with an unguarded look.

"You can," he said. "But don't ask if you don't want an honest answer, princess."

"It's not a serious question," she assured him, not wanting to mar the peace of the afternoon. "Well, maybe a little serious." She bit her thumb, second-guessing herself now that the words were on the tip of her tongue.

"Spit it out," he said, nudging her boot with his. "I won't bite. Not until we're back at the house, anyway."

The thought made an unhealthy wave of longing sizzle across her skin and she was suddenly shy about the nature of her question, but she pushed on anyway. "I was just wondering when you knew you were Dominant?" she asked, keeping her eyes on her sandwich. "Were you always that way or was it something someone taught you to enjoy?"

He hummed thoughtfully beneath his breath as he took another bite of his sandwich. She glanced over to find him gazing out at the sea, seeming to seriously consider her question.

"A little of both I guess," he finally said. "Control was always important in my family. I learned how valuable it was to possess and costly to lose at a young age. But I think the first time I realized I was turned on by it was when I used to play jewel thief with the little girl who lived next door. She would pretend to be a cat burglar and I was an American spy working for the CIA."

He smiled softly to himself. "There was nothing more exciting than catching her with a sack of her mother's jewelry and tying her to a tree."

The unexpected confession made her laugh. "That's cute. A little twisted, but cute."

"There was nothing twisted about it," he said, smile widening. "Laney enjoyed it. I could tell. Even back then."

His words made Hannah's thoughts turn back to the night she'd awoken with her arms tied above her head and Jackson hovering over her in the darkness, smelling like rain, sex, and temptation. The memory made her nipples tighten and a flush of arousal sweep through her.

"I bet you could," she murmured, reaching for the chilled bottle of guava juice, hoping it would cool her off.

"How about you?" he asked. "Did you ever live out those submissive fantasies of yours with anyone else?"

She swallowed the juice, grateful for the extra moment to think. She didn't know how Harley would have answered that—whether she had lovers before Jackson who were Dominant or not—but she figured she was safer sticking to her own truth. "No. There hasn't been anyone since we moved. At least, nothing serious. I dated a couple of men a few years ago, but I've been too busy for that kind of thing."

"Too busy for a fuck buddy?" He lifted one brow. "I find that hard to believe."

"It's the truth," she said. "Seems like we're both into honesty today."

He met her gaze and something flickered behind his eyes.

"What are you thinking?" she whispered, even though she knew she shouldn't push. She shouldn't crave the intimacy of knowing his thoughts any more than she should crave his touch. He was the enemy, but it was hard to remember that on such a seemingly normal afternoon, when she felt more like she was on a first date than enjoying a brief break in her captivity.

"I am very interested in honesty today," he said, his voice rough with an emotion she couldn't decipher. But it wasn't anger and whatever he was feeling made it impossible to pull her eyes away from his. "But this isn't the place for it. We should finish up and start back soon so we'll have time to clean up before dinner. The cook is making something special."

"Her name's Eva," Hannah whispered, feeling it needed to be said. Names were important. Names helped strangers become friends.

If only she could tell Jackson her real name.

She wondered what would happen, if maybe he would understand why she'd lied...

"I know," Jackson said, leaning closer. "But she wasn't supposed to tell you her name. She wasn't supposed to talk to you at all."

Fear whispered through Hannah's chest. "She was just being polite. She didn't say anything else, except that she didn't speak English. Please, forget I said anything. I don't want to get her in trouble."

Jackson reached up, grabbing the back of her braid and giving a gentle tug, forcing her to tilt her head back, bringing her lips closer to his. "If I didn't know better I would think you cared."

"I do care," she said, heart racing as Jackson's mouth moved closer and the spicy, masculine smell of him swept through her head.

"Maybe," he murmured. "Maybe you do."

Hannah's pulse stuttered and her lips burned. She was so certain he was going to kiss her—and so eager for the feel of his tongue stroking against hers—that when he suddenly pulled away her fluttering heart plummeted into her stomach, making it clench.

"You should eat," he said, motioning toward the lunch forgotten in her lap. "I don't want you giving out halfway down the mountain."

She reached for her sandwich with an unsteady hand. "It would take more than a missed meal. I'm tougher than I look."

"That's one thing I've never doubted," he said, the mixture of frustration and admiration in his voice making her unsure how to respond.

So she said nothing. She turned her attention to finishing her sandwich and juice and watching the waves curl into the rocks far below.

Silence fell between them once again, but it wasn't the same as the comfortable silence they'd enjoyed before.

This silence was electrified, simmering with potential. Something had been set in motion, something was going to happen that would change both of their fates. Hannah wasn't sure what it was, but she sensed it wouldn't be long before she found out. This might not be the place for honesty, but they would find that place soon and then truths would come out.

Maybe the entire truth.

Slowly but surely, being hated by the man next to her was becoming as unbearable as the thought of her and Sibyl ending up on the streets. There was always a chance that with a mixture of hard work and a little luck that she could claw her way to a better life for her tiny family of two.

But if she waited too long to tell Jackson that she wasn't the woman he'd hunted, there would be no redemption for either of them. There were some things in life that couldn't be forgiven or forgotten, paths taken deep into the woods from which there was no way back.

Now Hannah had to decide whether it was time to come clean before it was too late.

CHAPTER FOURTEEN

Jackson

It took less time to get down the mountain than it had to hike up. Harley tried to strike up a conversation several times, but each attempt died a swift, sudden death.

Jackson couldn't stomach small talk, but he couldn't start his honesty experiment until they were back at the house. If they started talking here in the woods and her answers didn't satisfy him, there would be no one to keep him from wringing her neck and burying her body in a shallow grave beside the trail. The servants wouldn't lift a finger to stop him if he decided to strangle her on the dining room table, but knowing there were other eyes and ears close by would help him exercise restraint.

He didn't want to hurt Harley—at least not to the point of killing her—but his control was fraying fast. She was making him feel things again, things he was certain he was incapable of feeling for any woman, let alone the woman who had ruined his life.

He hated her, but he had enjoyed her today. He enjoyed her smile and her laugh and the way she looked at him with that wistful expression, as if she were wondering what could have been, if things had ended differently six years ago. It was insane, but those damned looks of hers and everything else that had happened between them in the past week had him wondering if maybe there was some sort of explanation.

Maybe she'd been forced into her deception. Maybe she'd fallen in with bad people and ruining him had been her only way out. Maybe the thing with Clay had been a way to keep her sanity, soothing herself with one man while she prepared to destroy another, and his death was purely accidental.

He knew people who forced others into situations like that now. Drug dealers who forced their girlfriends to become drug mules. Bookies who cut off a little girl's fingers, one by one, when her father failed to pay his debts in a timely fashion. Fathers who sold their own daughters into sexual slavery to solidify an alliance with a rival cartel.

He had no idea where Harley had come from or who her parents were—not even the best intelligence men had been able to pinpoint her origins—but there was a chance she'd come from a rough home life. She could have been born into some dark vendetta against his family and had no choice but to play her part.

Six years ago Jackson hadn't been the kind of man who ended up on a hit list, but his father certainly was. Ian Hawke had more than his share of enemies, from former business partners he'd ruined, to politicians he'd blackmailed, to women he'd used and discarded with no concern for the hearts he'd broken. And if someone didn't know his father well, they might have thought the best way to get to Ian was through his son. Most parents would take on any amount of suffering if it meant sparing their children pain, and Ian Hawke did a decent imitation of being that sort of man when there were witnesses around to observe.

In truth, Ian was more concerned about the embarrassment of having a son in prison than the fact that Jackson had been convicted of a crime he didn't commit. Ian hadn't even bothered hearing Jackson's side of the story. As soon as the arrest hit the news, he'd publicly disowned his son and Jackson knew if he hadn't already reached the age when his trust fund was in his control, Ian would have confiscated that as well.

And without that start-up money, Jackson would never have been able to capitalize on the connections he'd made in prison or become the self-made criminal he was today. There would have been no way out for him, no future but scraping by working the kind of jobs convicts were allowed to work, lingering on the fringes of decent society.

Maybe Harley had been in a similar situation. Maybe she'd had no choice, no other way out. Maybe he at least owed her the chance to explain herself and say something more than "I'm sorry."

But even if she had an explanation and was truly sorry, did that go anywhere close to excusing what she'd done?

She'd framed an innocent man and gotten away with it. The fact that Jackson wasn't innocent anymore didn't matter. She had redefined his life and turned him into something the polar opposite of the rule-following, honor-bound, decorated Marine he'd once been.

Was there any way to get past that?

He didn't know, but it was time to put the games aside and cut to the heart of the matter. He would give her the chance to be honest and if she failed the test, they would move forward with a new set of rules, one that involved no kindness, no dignity, no rewards, and no mercy.

They arrived back at the house just as the

sun was setting. Jackson walked Harley to the sliding glass door to her room, but stopped on the patio, not following her inside.

"Are we still having dinner?" she asked, gazing anxiously up at him, making it clear she could sense that the unresolved shit between them was swiftly coming to a head.

"We are," he said, his voice scratchy with disuse. He hadn't spoken a word in well over an hour. He'd been too lost in thought. "You'll find a dress and new shoes in your closet. Meet me in the dining room when you're ready."

"All right." A smile flickered across her face only to disappear just as quickly. "Then I'll see you soon."

Jackson nodded before spinning on his heel and circling around the side of the house, heading toward the servants' quarters. He needed to speak with Adam before things went any further with Harley. He needed to be sure the alternative lodging arrangements for his prisoner were ready if they were needed.

There was a chance that he and Harley

would both be sleeping in her big bed tonight, but there was an equal chance that she would end the evening in accommodations more fitting for a monster.

Monsters didn't deserve clean sheets, a soft mattress, or second chances.

Monsters deserved pain and a strong cage to contain them while they suffered.

CHAPTER FIFTEEN

Hannah

Hannah showered quickly, but took the time to blow dry her hair and curl the ends into ringlets with the fat curling iron she found under the sink.

In addition to the stunning strapless red maxi dress, with layers of chiffon over-skirting she knew would become something magical in an ocean breeze, she'd found delicate gold sandals in just the right size and a bag of high-end make-up waiting for her in the closet. She wasn't sure who had chosen the clothes and cosmetics, but the dress fit her like a dream and the bronze and pink hues were the perfect shade for her skin.

By the time she was finished dressing, she barely recognized the woman staring back at her in the mirror. She was stunning, every bit as beautiful as Harley had ever been, but with a vulnerable look in her eyes that betrayed her swiftly softening heart.

It was time to face the truth. She wasn't her twin and she would never be hard enough or clever enough to pull off this kind of deception. Even if she could figure out exactly what Harley had done to Jackson, there was no guarantee she could find a way to make amends or help him heal. And she wanted to help him heal. The more time she spent with him, the more certain she became that he hadn't deserved what Harley had done to him, and it wasn't a side effect of Stockholm Syndrome to want to help a victim recover.

Sometime between this morning and tonight, she'd become certain that closing herself off wasn't the answer. She could fight the connection she felt to Jackson tooth and nail, but the end result would be the same.

She was going to keep falling for him, and continue to crave his touch until the day they put her in the ground. Her best chance of surviving with her heart and soul intact was to tell him the truth, the whole truth, and throw herself on his mercy.

He still had some left inside of him. There was a good man buried beneath the hardened mercenary. She had glimpsed it today and a dozen other times since they'd arrived on the island. Now she just had to hope there was enough of that good man left to forgive her for lying to him.

"All you can do is try," she whispered as she started down the hall from the bedroom. She walked through the now empty kitchen and into a stunning great room with vaulted ceilings, plush couches and chairs arranged in cozy conversational groupings, with a pool glittering at the center of the room.

It was a gorgeous space and for a moment she couldn't help imagining how much fun she and Jackson could have in a room like this if all the ugliness between them could be put away. Images of her kneeling at Jackson's feet by the pool, both of them naked in the water, or entwined on one of the soft couches flashed through her head, but she pushed the erotic images away. She had to keep her wits about her and dwelling on how much she wanted to be with Jackson—really be with him, not as Harley, but as herself—was the kind of distraction she didn't need.

Following the scent of something grilled and lovely smelling, she found her way into the dining room, but the large polished wood table was empty and the bay doors leading onto the front lanai were open. Outside on the redwood decking a table draped in white linen was set for two, with a gently sweating bottle of champagne, a water carafe filled with lemon slices, fresh flowers, and two silver dome covered plates.

But she couldn't focus on the lovely table for long, not when something far more beautiful stood on the other side, framed by two flickering tiki torches fitted into the lanai railing.

Jackson was facing the sliver of sea visible at the end of the lane, his broad shoulders relaxed and the wind ruffling his still damp hair. His white dress shirt and gray suit pants fit him perfectly, accentuating the power of the body beneath the elegant fabric. The contrast of the civilized clothing and the dangerous man who wore them was the sexiest thing she'd ever seen, reminding her that there were more barriers to a way forward for the two of them than the ugliness of the past.

This man was a criminal, an unrepentant predator, maybe even a killer.

But even as the thought flitted through her head, she dismissed it. She couldn't imagine Jackson killing. He'd said that he had respect for life. Just not hers.

Or not *Harley's*.

She pulled in an anxious breath, ready to get this over with, to scatter Jackson's expectations and see if there was anything left worth saving between them once he realized the truth. She crossed the freshly stained planks to stand at his elbow, feeling very small beside him. She barely came up to his shoulder. She hadn't noticed the height difference that much until now, when so much was riding on her being strong enough to find a way to get him to understand.

Swallowing past the lump in her throat she parted her lips to speak only to have Jackson turn to her and bring one finger to press against her mouth.

"Not yet," he said. "We'll get to that part, but first we're going to enjoy the food Eva prepared."

Holding his gaze, marveling at how much deeper she could see into his soft brown eyes, she nodded. They were going to tell the truth, both of them, but something unmistakable had already been confessed.

He felt the pull between them, too. He felt it, and perhaps once her true identity was revealed, he wouldn't feel the need to fight it.

"You're beautiful," he said, setting her nerves to tingling as he moved his hand from her mouth and stepped back to let his gaze drift up and down her body. "Perfect."

"You too," she said, shivering, amazed at how much he could make her feel with just a look.

"Cold?" He nodded toward the house. "We can go inside if you'd rather."

She shook her head. "No. I'm not cold. It's lovely out."

"Then we should eat while the food's warm," he said, leading the way to the table and pulling out her chair.

She settled in, the back of her neck prickling with awareness when Jackson's hands lingered on her bare shoulders for a moment before he circled around the table. On the way to his chair he plucked the silver cover from her plate and then his own, revealing a perfectly cooked medallion of filet mignon, surrounding by freshly grilled potatoes and vegetables.

At the sight of the steak she smiled. "I had a feeling you were a red meat kind of man."

"I thought we deserved something decadent." He sat, reaching for the champagne and pouring her a glass. "And this is part of your reward, after all. I assume you enjoy still-mooing meat as much as you used to."

She hesitated, torn between continuing the

ruse for a little longer and dropping her bomb now. But Jackson was right, they probably wouldn't have much of an appetite after the truth came out, at least not for a while, and she was starving, even if she had always preferred fish to red meat.

"Steak is perfect," she said. "Thank you."

"Then bon appetit, princess." He draped his napkin into his lap, claimed his silverware, and proceeded to dig into his meal with the grace of a man who was accustomed to eating in high-class restaurants with civilized people.

He was such an odd and compelling mixture of conflicting traits. It made her want to ask questions, get to know more about him.

And why shouldn't she? She was too close to sharing her secret to worry about giving herself away by asking things Harley should know.

"I know we're not talking about anything too serious until after dinner," she said, as her knife eased into her steak like the meat was made of melted butter. "But I'd love to know more about what you were like growing up.

What did you enjoy aside from playing jewel thief and CIA agent?"

Jackson shot her a skeptical look as he chewed, but when he'd swallowed his first bite, he replied more frankly than she'd expected. "I enjoyed soccer, football, chess, and staying out of my parents' way as much as possible. My mother didn't have much interest in parenting and my father and I didn't care for each other. That's why I applied to military boarding school as soon as I turned thirteen. And from there I went straight to West Point."

Her eyebrows lifted. "You went to West Point?"

"Graduated top of my class, and was one of only two graduates to be commissioned into the Marines instead of the Army." He frowned. "I'm sure I told you that the day we toured Quantico."

"I'm sorry, it must have slipped my mind," she lied, impressed. And even more confused. West Point and service in the Marines.

How had he gone from there to here?

"What about you," he said, stabbing

another bite of steak. "What were you like as a child? Aside from determined to change your name?"

She glanced down at her plate, cutting a slice of grilled zucchini in half. "Quiet. My sister did the talking for both of us. She was a natural leader and I was happy to follow. I guess I've always had that side of me. The part that prefers to let someone else lead." She glanced up at him through her lashes, as she added, "Though I can't say following my sister's charted course was always enjoyable."

He cocked his head, seemingly interested though his gaze was more guarded than it had been a moment before. "And why's that?"

"I got hurt a lot when I was following her orders," she said. "When I was younger I assumed she didn't think far enough ahead to realize the potentially dangerous consequences of her actions. But as we got older, I realized she just didn't care."

She lifted a shoulder as she reached for her glass of champagne, needing a little liquid courage as she skated closer to the truth. "I mean, I had it better than the friends or boyfriends who got in her way, but she was only protective of me to a point. After that, I was on my own."

"And where is she now? Still out there somewhere causing trouble?"

"She's dead." Hannah studied his expression, but his gentle nod gave nothing away.

"I'm sorry," he said. "I hear losing family can be hard."

"It is," she said, her tongue slipping out to dampen her lips. "It's even harder when they leave unfinished business behind. Messes you're left with that you can barely understand, let alone know how to clean up."

His brows drew together, but before he could respond something buzzed in his lap. He shifted his weight, pulling a cell from his front pocket and glancing quickly at the screen before he pushed his chair away from the table. "Excuse me, I have to take this. Business. But keep eating, no sense in both our dinners getting cold."

"Of course," Hannah said, heart thudding in her ears with a mixture of frustration and relief as Jackson disappeared though the doors leading into the dining room. She heard him say hello, but his next words faded away as he retreated deeper into the house.

Adrenaline pumped through her system, making her hands shake as she set her silverware down beside her plate. For a second, she'd thought he was about to put the pieces together, and a new fear had sliced through her head like a laser.

What if he didn't believe she was telling the truth about being Harley's identical twin? Considering everything he'd been through, he might be more inclined to think her "explanation" was just another lie. And how on earth would she prove otherwise? She had no pictures of her and Harley together, no birth certificate except the forgery she'd brought with her to Tahiti.

And what would he do to her then? When he was certain he couldn't trust a word out of her mouth?

She sensed it would be bad, and that she would suffer more for having made her way past his first line of defenses. He'd let her in today, more than he ever had before. If she betrayed what little trust he'd given her, he would make sure she suffered for it.

She had to make a decision. Right now. She might not get another chance to exercise her free will before Jackson took it away from her again.

As if summoned by her fearful thoughts, she caught sight of Adam on the far side of the lawn, emerging from one of the small huts she guessed were the servant's quarters. He had a phone pressed to his ear and was carrying a hefty kennel, the kind used for Labrador Retrievers or other large dogs.

But there were no large dogs on this island, no dogs at all as far as she knew. And certainly no reason for Adam to be carrying that kennel around to the back of the house— to where she had slept since she arrived on the island—except one.

The cage was for her.

For some reason—whether it was to be part of her and Jackson's "play" or something more serious—that cage was being taken to her room. Jackson didn't know that she suffered from claustrophobia and might not care if he did. It would all depend on whether she was speaking to kind Jackson or heartless Jackson and there were no guarantees which she would get.

They had no safe word, no contract drawn up to encourage him to respect her limits, and the man had contradicted himself more than once when it came to what she could expect if she resisted his control.

Once, he'd threatened to send her home on the next plane without another penny. But before that, he'd threatened to make her suffer if she tried to run. And why would he make a threat like that if he was truly willing to set her free?

It was suddenly starkly clear that she should be worrying far less about whether Jackson would believe her story and far more about whether she believed his.

The difference in focus could mean much more than the loss of a lover; it could mean the difference between life and death.

CHAPTER SIXTEEN

Jackson

Hiro's call came at the perfect time. Jackson needed a moment to clear his thoughts and refocus his intentions. He'd known Harley would be beautiful in that dress, but he hadn't been prepared for the sucker punch of desire that had nearly leveled him when he'd turned to see her standing next to him, looking up into his eyes like all she wanted in the world was to rewind the clock and go back to when they first met.

To go back and make things better, to give them a shot at having more than some intense hate fucking on the way to hell and back.

She'd taken his breath away. He'd wanted to take her right there on the lanai, shove her dress up and rip her panties down and fuck her from behind with the wind blowing that dress around their joined bodies as he made her come, screaming his name loud enough for the servants to hear. He wanted to fuck her until there were no more lies left between them, just the truth of how hot they were together, electric like nothing he'd ever known.

But instead, he'd forced himself to sit down and get something in his stomach before things got ugly.

And things were going to get ugly, he had no doubt about that. Nothing Hiro might have managed to learn in the past week would change that.

Jackson and Harley were on a collision course. The crash was inevitable. The only question that remained was whether there would be anything worth salvaging among the wreckage when it was over.

"All right, talk," Jackson said, closing the

door to his bedroom behind him. His room wasn't as large as Harley's, but it was big enough to provide plenty of room to pace while Hiro filled him in on the fruits of his first week of spying.

"Sibyl is very reluctant to talk about Hannah or the rest of the family, and shuts down whenever I push the subject," Hiro said. "I can't be certain, but I believe they've suffered a great loss and may even be in hiding from people who wish them ill."

Jackson's brows drew together, but he supposed it wasn't such a strange thing to hear. He might not be the only former victim of Harley's out looking for revenge.

"What else?" he demanded.

"Sibyl has nightmares," the pearl farmer said, affection and pity clear in his voice. "Her medications make it difficult for her to come fully awake during the night and leave the nightmares behind. She's called out several names during her sleep, but so far nothing that would aid in the discovery of another last name. If there is one."

"There is one, I'm certain of it," Jackson

said, pacing back toward the bedroom door. "Is there anything else or should I look for someone who will make sure I get what I pay for."

"Don't send anyone else," Hiro said, pitch rising. "I'm making progress, I just need more time. I found a letter Hannah wrote as a child and an old photograph yesterday. I took pictures of them with my phone so I could send them to you. There may be more keepsakes that will offer clues, but Sibyl woke up from her nap before I could find them."

Jackson fought the urge to curse. It wasn't Hiro's fault. He'd had private detectives on retainer who had found out less than the farmer had. Sibyl was every bit as secretive and mysterious as her niece. "Fine, send me the images and look harder this week. I'll have Adam make a deposit to your account."

"I don't need the deposit," Hiro said, cutting in before Jackson could hang up on him. "I'll help so that you won't have to hire some stranger to bother Sibyl, but I don't want any more of your money. I don't want to have that hanging over my head. She means something to me."

"Congratulations," Jackson said, but his sneer wasn't as pronounced as it would have been a week ago.

All the more reason to finish this call and get back to Harley. He had to know if she was making a fool of him all over again or if there was something real growing between them, no matter how twisted its origins or tangled its roots.

Jackson ended the call with Hiro and waited for the text to come through—wanting to review all the information before he returned to Harley—but he didn't expect a child's letter or the picture to offer any real insight. It wasn't until the image flashed onto his screen that he realized what was wrong about Hiro discovering a letter "Hannah" had written when she was a child.

There was no Hannah, not until six years ago when Harley Garrett became Hannah North.

Or at least that's what he'd thought...

He gazed down at the faded picture of the two little girls in front of a sparkling lake, his stomach turning as the truth of what he was seeing penetrated.

The brown-haired, ponytailed girls were maybe ten or eleven years old. The slightly smaller, skinnier one stood with her foot propped up on a beached canoe and her hands fisted on her hips, silently daring the world to prove she wasn't the master of all she surveyed. The more solid of the two, stood slightly back from her sister, watching her other half with a big grin on her face. She was so caught up in enjoying whatever joke had just been told that she didn't seem to notice the camera, which only made the image more poignant.

Both of the girls were lovely—mirror images so alike he doubted their own mother could tell them apart without looking very closely—but the second girl's smile made her loveliness something more. Something sweet and touching and terribly familiar.

He'd seen the same smile beaming up at him for half the hike this afternoon.

A moment later, a shot of the back of the photo came through with "Harley and

Hannah Grade 5" scrawled in looping script, but by that point he'd already sorted out the truth.

Harley had a twin sister. A twin.

And Jackson had most likely spent the past week alternatively tormenting and fucking the wrong woman.

A thousand questions dumped into his head all at once—Why had she lied? Why had she allowed things to go so far? Was she protecting Harley? Was Harley even still alive?

Or had the past five years been a wild goose chase that ended now, with him realizing he'd committed the same sin he'd hated Harley for?

Had he been punishing an innocent woman for a crime she didn't commit?

No one is innocent.

But looking at that little girl's smile the words didn't feel as true as they did even a week ago.

He didn't take the time to read the letter scrawled in a child's handwriting that appeared on the screen after the front and back of the photo. He turned and stalked across the room, hurried through the open living area where the softly whirring fans above his head seemed to mock him for being a fucking fool, and took the five steps up into the dining room at a run.

But when he stepped out onto the lanai, Harley—Hannah's?—chair was empty and her napkin blowing across the wooden planks in the ocean breeze.

She was gone.

But she wouldn't get far.

man picked up. "Our guest decided to make a break for her freedom while I was inside taking a phone call. She doesn't have more than a ten-minute head start. Fetch the gardener and start looking down toward the beach. I'll check the road back toward town."

"Yes, sir," Adam said, hanging up without bothering to say goodbye.

Slipping his phone back into his pocket, Jackson turned and started walking up the road toward town, carefully scanning the ground for signs of which way his prey had run.

He was going to find her, and then, one

way or another, he was going to force the truth out of her pretty mouth and find out everything she'd been hiding.

To be continued…

Jackson and Hannah's story continues in
DESPERATE DOMINATION
Available Now.

Acknowledgements

First and foremost, thank you to my readers. Every email and post on my Facebook page has meant so much. I can't express how deeply grateful I am for the chance to entertain you.

More big thanks to my Street Team, who I am convinced are the sweetest, funniest, kindest group of people around. You inspire me and keep me going and I'm not sure I'd be one third as productive without you. Big tackle hugs to all.

More thanks to Kara H. for organizational excellence and helping me get the word out. (No one would have heard of the books without you!) Thanks to the Facebook groups who have welcomed me in, to the bloggers who have taken a chance on a newbie, and to everyone who has taken time out of their day to write and post a review.

And of course, many thanks to my husband, who not only loves me well, but also supports me in everything I do. I don't know how I got so lucky, man, but I am hanging on tight to you.

Tell Lili your favorite part!

I love reading your thoughts about the books and your review matters. Reviews help readers find new-to-them authors to enjoy. So if you could take a moment to leave a review letting me know your favorite part of the story—nothing fancy required, even a sentence or two would be wonderful—I would be deeply grateful.

About the Author

Lili Valente has slept under the stars in Greece, eaten dinner at midnight with French men who couldn't be trusted to keep their mouths on their food, and walked alone through Munich's red light district after dark and lived to tell the tale.

These days you can find her writing in a tent beside the sea, drinking coconut water and thinking delightfully dirty thoughts.

Also By Lili Valente

Standalones

The Baby Maker

The Troublemaker

The Bad Motherpuckers Series

Hot as Puck

Sexy Motherpucker

Puck-Aholic

Puck me Baby

Sexy Flirty Dirty Romantic Comedies

Magnificent Bastard

Spectacular Rascal

Incredible You

Meant for You

The Master Me Series

(Red HOT erotic Standalone novellas)

Snowbound with the Billionaire

Snowed in with the Boss

Masquerade with the Master

Bought by the Billionaire Series

(HOT novellas, must be read in order)

Dark Domination

Deep Domination

Desperate Domination

Divine Domination

Kidnapped by the Billionaire Series

(HOT novellas, must be read in order)

Filthy Wicked Love

Crazy Beautiful Love

One More Shameless Night

Under His Command Series

(HOT novellas, must be read in order)

Controlling her Pleasure

Commanding her Trust

Claiming her Heart

To the Bone Series

(SRomantic Suspense, must be read in order)

A Love so Dangerous

A Love so Deadly

A Love so Deep

Run with Me Series

(Emotional New Adult Romantic Suspense.
Must be read in order.)

Run with Me

Fight for You

The Bad Boy's Temptation Series

(Must be read in order)

The Bad Boy's Temptation

The Bad Boy's Seduction

The Bad Boy's Redemption

Learn more at www.lilivalente.com

Printed in Great Britain
by Amazon